Monica Hughes

The Isis Pedlar

HAMISH HAMILTON: LONDON

First published in Great Britain 1982 by
Hamish Hamilton Children's Books
Garden House 57–59 Long Acre London WC2E 9JZ

Copyright © 1982 by Monica Hughes

British Library Cataloguing in Publication Data

Hughes, Monica
The Isis pedlar
I. Title
823′.914[J]   PZ7

Hamish Hamilton ISBN 0-241-10834-9

First published in Canada 1982 by
Fleet Publishers, a division of International Thomson Limited
1410 Birchmont Road, Scarborough, Ontario, Canada M1P 2E7

Fleet Publishers ISBN 0-7706-0036-0

Photoset, printed and bound in Great Britain

Chapter One

The Luck of the Irish burst out of hyperspace like a squeezed grape seed. Klaxons shrieked. Bells rang. The bulkheads of the old space ship groaned.

"Oh, saints protect us!" Michael Joseph Flynn picked himself up off the floor. "Oh, me poor head!"

Moira Flynn reached the control panel, stilled the klaxons and silenced the bells. She peered at the view screen, her heart pounding. It was reassuringly black, pinpointed with distant stars. At least it seemed that they hadn't entered real space in the grip of a black hole or within spitting distance of a star.

She scanned three hundred and sixty degrees and her heart jumped. It had been close enough. Twenty degrees off their starboard bow blazed a sun, its small disc a hot blue-white. Carefully Moira set the controls so that *The Luck of the Irish* fell into a wide orbit around this unknown sun. Then she sighed with relief and swung the captain's chair round.

"Are you all right then, Dad?"

"All right? Of course I'm not all right. I think I've broken me poor head."

"Oh, it can't be that bad. You're sitting up and talking." Moira picked her way across the littered control room and helped him to his feet. "Come on then. Sit down there and I'll have a look."

She soothed him, got ice from the aged refrigerator and put a pillow behind his head. "Better now, Dad?"

1

"You're a good girl, Moira. Now just pour a small tot for your Dad. Me nerves are jangling like an old harp."

"It says in the first-aid book that you should never take alcohol after a head injury. I'll make you a nice cup of tea."

"I don't want a cup of tea. I want some whiskey." The lines from his thin nose to his mouth deepened into peevish furrows. Moira sighed and he sensed her weakening. "Just a small tot. For me heart, dear girl. Me heart and me nerves."

Moira dug a key out of her overall pocket, unlocked one of the many cupboards that lined the room, and pulled out a bottle. As he watched her pour the amber liquid into a glass the lines left Mike's face and it became as smooth as a child's.

"There's me good girl. Just the one tot." He tossed it back without a blink and licked his lips. "And one more to sip before you put away the bottle." He held out the empty glass.

"Oh, Mike, what am I going to do with you?" She filled the glass and turned away to lock up the bottle. She put the key carefully back in her pocket.

Mike Flynn began to toss back the second tot, and then remembered that he had to make it last. A hard woman his daughter was turning into, he thought. Not like her blessed mother, who had never said 'No' to Mike from the day they first met in the bar on Altarius Two until her death from pneumonia eleven years later.

Moira picked her way across the room and squatted down by the control panel. She took a screwdriver from her belt and began to work. "When you've finished that drink, Mike," she said over her shoulder, "will you pick that stuff off the floor and stow it away? Else something's going to get broke or lost for sure."

"Maybe a little later, me love. I think I'll just rest me head for a minute or two."

A tiny sigh of exasperation escaped Moira. She tried to breathe it back in, feeling cross and disloyal at the same time. Why had she even bothered to ask? She knew she would be the one who would have to tidy up the ship.

2

Behind the control panel a module dark with carbon told the story. She pulled it out and looked at it gloomily. Two weeks' work—maybe more. And that would only be a patch-up job, enough to get them back into hyperspace and over to a more civilized sector of the Galaxy, where she'd be able to pick up a replacement. And how to pay for it, dear knows, she thought, and sighed again.

She put the fused module down on the table and turned to fiddle with the view screen controls, trying to match up the star patterns out there with the computer's memory. Nothing seemed to work. Her throat tightened with panic and she swung her chair round to face her father.

"We're lost, Mike! This old tub of yours has finally given up and dumped us, and I haven't the faintest idea where."

"Of course you have, me darling. You know where we came from and where we're heading. Stands to reason that we're somewhere betwixt the two. That shouldn't be so hard to work out."

Anger pushed away Moira's fear. "You never listen and you'll never learn, will you, Dad? I've told you over and over. Hyperspace is bent. It's not like ordinary space at all. More like those crazy mirrors at the Galactic Fair on Denebon Five. Remember? If we've popped out of hyperspace in the middle of one of those crazy curves we could be anywhere in the Galaxy, anywhere at all."

"Well, can you fix the hyperdrive?"

"I don't know. Maybe. I think so. But there's no point fixing the drive if we don't know where we are and where we're going. Next time we might not be so lucky. We could have popped out in the middle of a sun. This old tub!"

"You'll manage," Mike said comfortably.

Moira's eyes stung. She longed to have someone to hold her in his arms and tell her that everything was all right and that she'd never have to worry about anything ever again. It's not fair, she thought, blinking back angry tears. I'm fifteen, and I'm old. *Old*. I've never once had a chance to be just a kid and now I never will. I'm so scared, and *he* won't lift a finger to help. I don't know how to get us out of this mess. The dear Lord knows I've got us out of many, from one end of the Galaxy to t'other. But I'm defeated now, I'm beat.

She slumped back in the contoured control chair. The plastic cover had long ago split, and the padding showed through, dirty grey. She sniffed and then blew her nose. From the other end of the cabin came a gentle snore. The battered old *The Luck of the Irish* slowly orbited the unknown star. It would orbit it for ever unless she made up her mind to do something and then did it.

The unknown star—that was the place to start! Spectral analysis. Temperature. Diameter. Mass. If she could match up the facts with some known stars the computer could compare the background sky and tell her which was the right one. The computer was a sadly out-of-date model, but at least it could do *that*. She sat up straight and began to punch buttons and make notes. Soon she was singing under her breath.

Twenty-eight minutes later the computer hiccoughed and spat out an answer. The unknown F5 star was called Ra. It was situated five parsecs from Earth in the direction of the constellation Indus. It had a mass one and a third times that of the Sun and was two and a half times as bright. That was all the old computer could tell her. The rest she could get from Blackie's *Galactic Guide*.

Mike was still snoring. His puckish face was bland and unlined in sleep, his fair hair pushed back from his high forehead by the icepack. With his eyes shut he looked poetically beautiful, young and feckless.

Why do I put up with his nonsense? Moira asked herself. On and on through space, never staying long enough on a planet to begin to call it home . . .

She sat on the floor to sort out the books and charts that had spewed out of the cupboard. That faulty latch. She'd asked him to fix it, over and over.

4

There it was—Blackie's *Galactic Guide*. Bother! Only Volume One: Abaran to Menorab. It took her ten more minutes to find Volume Two, wedged under the captain's chair.

Ra . . .Ra . . . There it was! Mass, diameter, luminosity. All checked with the computer readings. It had ten planets, five of them rocky, five gaseous. The fourth was habitable, after a fashion.

She scrambled up from the floor and, still reading, walked back to her chair. Fourth planet: Isis. Mean distance from Ra: 225 million kilometres. Gravitational pull at the surface: ·88 that of Earth, comfortable enough. Less good were the high ultra-violet radiation and a low-oxygen atmosphere. Further down the page she read that 'life is comfortable in the extensive rift-valley systems, supportive equipment necessary on the heights'. At the end an asterisk led her to a footnote . . . 'See Blackie's *List of Colonized Planets*.'

"Glory be!" Moira jumped to her feet and shook her father. "Mike! Wake up, will you!"

"What? Are we foundering then?"

"No, no. Oh, Dad, you'll never believe it, but your Irish luck's come up again. There's an Earth colony down there!"

"Bless us all!" He sat up and threw the icepack on the floor. "Where's Blackie's *List*? I've homework to do." He rubbed his hands together and his pale eyes shone.

"It's down on the floor some place, Dad."

"What a terrible mess! Could you not have been tidying it up a little while I was recovering from me injury? Oh, well, seems I must do it myself if I want it done."

He began to go through the stuff on the floor, reading titles and throwing the books to one side, so that the mess was worse than when he'd begun. In the end Moira took each discarded volume from him and put it in its right place in the cupboard. She smiled as she worked. She couldn't help it. They were no longer lost in galactic emptiness. And Dad was happy. His mind was working busily, and before

5

long he would begin to weave a delightful web of confusion to snare the innocent and unsuspecting inhabitants of Isis. He was in control.

"Ha!" He pounced and held up a book triumphantly. "Now we'll see what's what." He riffled through the pages. "Isis. Fourth planet of Ra. Coordinates—and so on and so on. Well, we'll not be needing these since we're already here. Colonized from earth in 2081 Earth Orbit Year . . ." he stopped.

Moira looked up. His lips were moving and there was a curious expression on his face. Then he slammed the book shut and stuffed it in his pocket. "Well then, I'll be getting down to the fine print later. Right now I'm starving for a good meal and me poor brain won't work at all."

"Mike Flynn, what's in that book?"

"Not a thing that would take your fancy, I promise you. Tell you what, this is a fine occasion for a feast. Why don't I whip up one of me specials?"

"Mike! What's in that book? There's something wrong with Isis, isn't there? Something you don't want me to know about. Isn't that the truth of it?"

"There's not a solitary blessed thing wrong, me darling. I swear it on the grave of me own dear mother." He looked at her, his eyes wide and innocent, very pale and flat. Sometimes his eyes seemed to have no depth to them at all, like shallow water over stones. She knew he was lying.

"All right then, Dad." She tried to smile. "You do the cooking, and I'll finish tidying up in here. And this time *I'll* fix the darn latch on the cupboard door."

By the time she had finished Mike had produced an extravagant feast out of their dwindling supplies—they had left Brown's Planet in considerable haste with the police on their tail, and no time to stock up. She guessed that there must be plenty of food on Isis, but he wouldn't tell her a thing about what he'd read, only filled the next few hours with zany jokes and reminiscences about the places they'd

6

seen and the narrow escapes they'd had. He turned it all into such a joke that Moira couldn't help laughing with him, though she remembered well that at the time it had been just awful, one step ahead of the police all the way.

He sent her off to bed early, and when she woke up again he was waiting impatiently for her, rocking from the balls of his feet to his heels and back again. He was a little red-eyed and he hadn't shaved, but otherwise you'd never guess that he'd spent all the sleep hours 'studying'. Working out a new caper, Moira thought, and wondered what the police were like on Isis.

"Will you put us in a nice orbit around Isis, me dear, so I can have a closer look? I've a mind to go down and visit these fine people."

Hold on to your gold and silver, Moira thought. Not to mention the fillings in your teeth. For this Irish pedlar of mine will charm them right out of your heads. But she did as Mike told her, and brought *The Luck of the Irish* spiralling inward to orbit the fourth planet.

"It doesn't look like much." She peered at the screen. "Considering it's been colonized since 2081." The wrinkled red surface passed beneath them. All mountainous. The only other colour was a blue-green stain that defined the wrinkles . . . the rift-valley system, she guessed. Then a sudden dazzle of blue made her blink. A great ocean, half a planet wide. They plunged into the darkness of night-side. The blackness was absolute. No lights. No cities. No signs of industry . . .

"No one's home. Nothing for you here, Mike."

"You must let your old Dad be the judge of that, me dear."

"What *was* in Blackie's *Planets* then?"

"Never bother your pretty head about that."

"*Mike!*"

They were racing over the twilight zone now, and Mike leaned forward, his finger on the screen. "Give me a synchronous orbit over that big valley system down there.

7

D'you see it, running north and south there?"

"There's nothing down there, Mike."

"Oh, I've a fancy to stretch me legs."

"We ought to repair the hyperdrive before we go down, Dad. Suppose we have to leave in a hurry."

"Oh, you know I'm not the least bit of good with me hands. I'll just be in your way. Give me that orbit over the valley and I'll hop on down and take a bit of a look around while you fix the drive. I'll be back in a jiffy. You'll never know I'm gone."

"Dad! what kind of a jiffy?"

"A couple of days. Well, no more than a week or so, I promise. It'll take you that long to fix the drive, won't it?"

"At least that. It's an awful mess." Moira sighed impatiently. "Oh, Dad, it would serve you right if I blinked into hyperspace and left you here."

"Oh, you'd never do that. You'd never leave your old Dad. You know I couldn't manage at all without you."

And that's God's truth, she thought, as she drifted *The Luck of the Irish* into an orbit that placed them safely out of the way of Isis' two tumbling little moons, a synchronous orbit which left them apparently hovering over the rift-system that Mike had pointed out. From this height it was a grey-green thread against the reddish mountain mass.

"If you're not back by the time I've repaired the unit I'll come down to get you," she warned him. She turned from the controls to face him and her mouth fell open. "Lord help us, will you look at yourself!"

"Grand, isn't it?" His pale eyes twinkled. Mischief seemed to spring from his finger-tips like static electricity. He was dressed in doublet and tights of gold and red, with a cloak lightly caught at the shoulders with brooches that winked with bright stones.

Denebon Five, Moira remembered. Conned off that unsuspecting miner in a game of chance that hadn't a speck of chance in it—though the miner didn't realise it until *The*

Luck of the Irish was clearing the landing field. The cloak was red, lined with the delicate green fur of moon-mink from Kator's Planet. A prince's fortune, it was worth.

"Well, you look as fine as fivepence, there's no doubt about it. But who'll you be showing it to? And how long will those fine shoes last on the rocks down there? And what about the oxygen and the ultra-violet?"

"There's oxygen in the flyer and I've got me pills. As for me shoes, I'm not planning to mountaineer, but I've got me force field and that'll keep off the shock of sticks and stones, not to mention the ultra-violet. So stop fussing over me like an old granny, will you now?" He touched the jewelled belt that fastened his doublet and flourished the little cane he held in his left hand. "Better than a brolly in the rain is me force field."

"Oh, Dad, be careful!" It burst out of her, though she hadn't meant to say a thing.

He waved a casual hand and stepped into the airlock. Two minutes later one of the two flyers dropped from its pod and glided down towards the tiny grey-green thread of life on the planet below. She saw the spark of its brake jets and then it spiralled out of sight.

The Luck of the Irish seemed very empty and even shabbier than usual now Mike was gone. When he was there his talk could charm away reality, so that you only saw what he wanted you to see. But now . . .

Moira looked around the control room and sighed. It was cramped and dingy. The paint had flaked off the bulkheads, the upholstery was split, the plastic instrument indicators were yellowed and scratched. If only they could stay in one place long enough for a refit. If only they had enough money to *pay* for a refit. If only . . .

She shook her head, cleared a space for herself at the table, and settled down to the painstakingly slow job of repairing the fused hyperdrive module. Between whiles, as she rested her eyes from the microscopic work, she thought about

9

Mike and wondered what he was up to this time.

It had been on Wallania that Mother had died. Of pneumonia, after being soaked to the skin and hanging around in Wallania's icy winds, while Mike wound up a caper that netted him fifty gold pieces and two firestones. She had caught the ten-year-old Moira's hands between her two burning ones.

"Look after him," she'd told the child. "Look after Mike . . ." Then she had died. No antibiotics on Wallania, and the first-aid kit hadn't been replenished from whichever place they'd left in a hurry before.

It should have been the other way round, Moira thought now, with a twinge of resentment. Mother should have made *him* promise to look after *me*. But then she'd been married to him for eleven years, hadn't she? She knew . . .

It took three weeks of hard work and ingenious making-do to mend the module and test it out as well as she could. The real test would come when they actually went into hyperdrive, riding the roller coaster peaks and troughs of warped space.

She went to the radio to talk to Mike and tell him to come back. It was only then, when she was still on open channel, that she found the second-stage condenser was missing. Not damaged, as the hyperdrive had been, from age and neglect, but missing, as in neatly removed and probably in Mike's pocket this very minute.

She had spare radio parts, of course. He must have known that, so why had he done it? It was stupid, infantile. Not like Mike at all. She found the replacement in her neat storage, connected the power supply again, and was just about to switch from open band reception to their two-way channel, when a voice startled her into a cry.

This is Isis. Coordinates X 123.491, Y 45.382, Z 157.905.
Keep your distance. Do not enter parking orbit.
Do not land.

Repeat: DO NOT LAND.

Interstellar quarantine conditions in effect.

Original Earth population in Primitive Agricultural Phase.

Not to be disturbed.

Repeat: NOT TO BE DISTURBED.

The metallic voice paused. The message was repeated. And again. Moira switched off. A looped tape beamed up to passing ships then. She wondered for how many years it had been running.

Oh, Mike, you wretch! You absolute wretch! So that was the secret of Isis that he'd found in Blackie's *List of Colonized Planets*. No wonder he hadn't let her read it! As if she'd ever have given him an orbit if she'd known that this place was quarantined. Oh, Michael Flynn, you've gone altogether too far this time, you really have!

She punched the broadcast button viciously. Oh, she'd burn his ear-drums, she would. She'd flay the skin off him!

She sat at the radio console for a full hour, but she couldn't raise him. Either he's dead or in jail, she thought. Or else he's in such deep mischief that he doesn't want me interfering. And that's the most likely answer. So quarantine or no quarantine, I'm going to have to go down to Isis myself and find the wretched man!

Chapter Two

If it had been anyone else seeing Mike Flynn land his flyer
on the top of Lighthouse Mesa, maybe things would have
turned out differently. But it was David N'Kumo, returning
late from hunting across the valley.

He stopped and stared while the evening breeze chilled
the sweat on his face and body and the weight of his game
bag cut into his shoulder. Above the Mesa a huge gold bird
glided stiffly down out of the sky and circled twice before
landing on the top of the Mesa. What could it be? He had
never seen anything like it before and he knew it did not
belong to the valley. Either it was a relic of the Old Times,
or he had had a glimpse of the spirit things beyond World's
End.

He shivered and broke into a run, his heart pounding. He
must tell the Council. The Council would understand what
he had seen and would know what should be done about it.

Then he imagined himself standing before Roger London,
telling him about a gold bird as large as a house. He broke
stride, stumbled and halted. Would they ever believe him?

"The N'Kumos again. It must be in the blood!" He could
hear President London's self-important voice and the
obedient laughter of the Council.

So he walked slowly the rest of the way back to the
village, and he said nothing to the kitchen aunties when he
left his game bag in the larder, and he was silent all through

supper. Afterwards he stood outside and stared up at the Mesa. It looked the same as always, a steep-sided squat shape that sprang from the valley floor like a surprise, dark against the darkening sky.

Maybe he should tell Uncle Jody what he'd seen. Uncle Jody understood what it was to be young and full of questions, to feel that there must be more to Isis than hunting, fishing and farming in this one valley for ever. Uncle Jody would believe him, even though what he'd seen was impossibly strange, for he too had had adventures and seen strange things and could tell stories about the world beyond the valley.

But nobody listened to Uncle Jody's stories, that was the trouble. And for years he had been silent. Perhaps he'd better not even tell Uncle Jody. After all, he was married now and had four small children of his own. The story of his banishment for sacrilege and his return from the land of That Old Woman had almost been forgotten. He would let Uncle Jody live in peace and not go stirring up any fire-ants' nests.

Just before bed David crept out again into the star-crowded night, and stared up at the black starless patch that was the shape of the Mesa. Was the spirit bird still roosting up there? Or had it left as silently as it had come?

For an eye-blink he thought he saw a light shine, as if through the frame of a window, halfway up the black shadowy shape. But then it was gone, and he wondered if he'd ever seen it. Had he even seen the bird? He went back to his house full of doubt and turmoil.

In the house carved long ago within the rock, halfway between the valley and the sky, Michael Joseph Flynn made himself snug. In the old records of the original settler ship, set down in Blackie's *Planets*, he had read of this tidy little house, and had seen at once that it would be the perfect place for his headquarters on Isis.

He planned to spend a day or two studying the history of

13

the early days of this planet, and at the same time keep an eye on what was going on nowadays down in the valley. He laid out a bedroll in the kitchen—the furniture in the other rooms had fallen into dust and decay. I'll have a fine feast and finish it off with a tot or two of the real stuff, he thought, and chuckled at the way in which he'd smuggled it off the ship right under the eyes of his daughter.

By the light of his energy pack he picked his way across the ruin of the living room and stood by the window looking down at the village below. A pretty place! His heart went out to its ignorant naïve farmers and their wives and children, all of them quietly preparing for sleep, quite unaware of the enormous exciting possibilities for their future that *he* would show them.

Three days later seven children playing stone-hops in the river above the lake saw a small, slim stranger walk jauntily down the river bank towards them, coming, it seemed, from the Cascades and the forbidden world beyond. They stared with open mouths, and stared again at his appearance.

You would have expected him to be ragged and dusty, panting for air after his climb down from the heights. But no. He was as neat and dapper as a calico-bird, dressed in close-fitting jacket, breeches and stockings, all woven of a beautiful red shot through with gold, so that the morning light made him shimmer from head to toe. On his head was a cap with the jauntiest of feathers stuck in it, that bobbed up and down as he walked. Thrown carelessly back from his shoulders, as if it were of no importance at all, was a wonderful great cloak of red lined with green fur.

The boys stared. The girls looked at their homespun skirts and pinafores, their knitted stockings and homemade leather sandals, and felt, for the first time in their lives, plain and ugly.

The stranger did not come right up to them, but bowed jauntily and sat down on a rock a little way off. He didn't say a word, but he picked up a flat stone and casually spun it downstream, hop, hop, hop, across the top of the waves, more hops even than Lars Holmstrom who was the very best.

The children came closer. The stranger picked up three pebbles and began to throw them up in the air and catch them again. Then he scooped up a fourth pebble. A fifth. A sixth. It was impossible, but they saw it with their own eyes. Then he waved his hand and the pebbles all disappeared into the air.

"Oh!" They all gasped. Now they were standing around his knees.

The stranger looked unsmilingly at each of them, and they all stared solemnly back. Very slowly his eyebrows went up, his eyes crossed and his ears wiggled. The tension broke and they laughed and pushed as close as they could get.

Marianne Oluk got up the nerve to reach out and touch the fur of the stranger's cloak. It was soft, softer even than purple-furs. She stroked it gently. She was small and plump and freckled.

"Do you like it?" The stranger spoke to *her*.

She nodded. The feelings inside made her afraid that she might burst if she said anything out loud.

"'Tis a gift from a king in a far, far country," he said, in a voice that was like singing, not flat and heavy like the way the valley people talked. "Have you ever seen fur to compare with it?"

Marianne shook her head. She swallowed and then whispered. "In the valley are purple-furs. Their coats are almost as soft as this, but purple, not green."

"Is that so indeed?" He seemed so impressed that Marianne blushed, shy and yet triumphant. He had spoken first to *her* and she had actually spoken back.

Now everyone began to talk at once, wanting to tell the stranger all the marvels of their valley and the good things that were in it.

15

He put his hands over his ears. "Oh, me poor head! I've been alone so long that my ears are not used to your pretty voices, chattering away like birds in an aviary."

"What's an aviary?"

"Why, it's a big cage for keeping birds in."

"Why should anyone want to do that? Poor birds."

"Don't you like to listen to birdsong then?"

"Of course." All the children nodded.

"Especially the mountain lark," added Marianne shyly. "Its song is so sweet. But it's very shy so you don't get to hear it often."

"If you caught your mountain larks and put them in an aviary, why, you could listen to their song whenever you chose to, just as if you were the king of the birds."

"How can anyone catch a *lark*?" Lars pushed forward. He didn't much like this stranger, showing off and making more stone-hops than he could.

The man leaned forward until his face was close to Lars'. He had smooth pink cheeks without a beard or bristle on them, but his hair was shoulder-length and straw-coloured. He stared into Lars' eyes with eyes that were pale and flat, so you couldn't see into them the least bit. Lars went to draw back, but the stranger caught him by the shoulders.

"Shall I give *you* the secret of how to trap a lark?" he asked softly. "Only you, and none of the others?"

Lars nodded vigorously.

"Well then, maybe I will, my fine fellow. And would you be liking a hat with a feather in it like mine?"

Lars nodded again and his eyes shone greedily.

"But that's cruel," Marianne interrupted.

The stranger's mouth smiled, though his eyes, still fixed on Lars, did not smile. "Oh, sure and we'll only be taking the feathers when the birds are through with them, me darling," he said lightly, and went on talking to Lars.

"You're a fine big upstanding fellow. What's your name now? . . . Lars? Why, you must be the leader here, Lars."

16

"Leader?"

"The boss. The one who decides what games to play and where you'll go. The one who settles arguments."

"Me?" Lars was doubtful.

The stranger slapped him on the shoulder. "Well, anyway, I appoint you leader. Then I can tell you secrets and you may share them with the others—if you choose." The flat grey eyes stared into Lars'.

He wriggled uncomfortably. "But . . ."

"Or I could choose one of the others . . ."

"Sure I'm the leader," Lars said in a rush.

"That's not fair," Grant Logan pushed forward. "How about me? I'm as old as Lars."

"Oh, I'll make it fair in a jiffy. Put up your hands if you want Lars to be your leader. Come on then, kids. Up with your hands. That's the way. Right. Lars is unanimously and democratically elected as leader."

The children stared at each other, impressed with the long words and the hand ceremony. This interesting man was talking to them just as if they were adults instead of no-accounts.

From his perch on the rock the stranger looked thoughtfully down at them. Then he slipped a satchel from his shoulder, and from the satchel drew a small bag. And from the bag a shining many-coloured globe. Was it a stone? Never had they seen anything so beautiful!

He held it up between finger and thumb—it was not much bigger than a fat summer-berry—and turned it so that they could see, trapped within it, all the colours of Ra's bow. They were still staring when he waved his other hand, and behold, the stone vanished.

"Oh!" They groaned and stared at his empty hand. He leaned over to Grant Logan and pulled his ear. And there was the magic globe again! They all saw it fall right out of Grant's ear into the stranger's hand. Grant stopped sulking and turned bright red. He put his hand up to his ear.

17

Carelessly, as if it were of no value at all, the stranger dropped the magic stone into Grant's hand. "There. It is yours. Will you do something for me?"

"To be sure, sir." Grant's eyes bulged. His fingers closed tightly over the stone.

"Will you tell the leader of this place that Michael Joseph Flynn would like to meet him and have a word or two."

"If you come with me I'll take you to him."

"No, no. I'll just stay here until I'm invited," he said humbly, as if he were a person of no importance.

Grant turned and ran towards the village. The stranger looked about him in an approving way, as if he couldn't have picked a nicer place to spend a day. Ra was high above the eastern mountains by now, and heat shimmered off the rocky floor of the river valley, but in spite of his fur cloak the stranger seemed comfortable.

After a while he reached into his satchel and pulled out a cup. "Who'll give me a drink for another magic stone?" he asked.

"Why would a cup of water cost anything?" Marianne asked, and she took the cup from him and filled it carefully from the river, handing it back brimming with bubbly ice-cold water.

He took it from her with a bow that made her blush uncomfortably. In a way it was nice to be treated as a grown-up, and yet it made her feel silly, as if the stranger were only playing.

He drank from the cup, shook it dry and stowed it away again. "Ah, that was a grand drink, thank you, child." He gave Marianne another magic stone.

She stared at the pattern, a swirl of blue and green, as if the river had been captured inside the little ball. "But it was nothing. I was glad to give you a drink."

"You're too simple, child. You must learn to value yourself and what you do for others. Keep the marble."

"Thank you, sir." When you turned it the insides seemed

to move and change. It was the most beautiful thing in the whole world. But . . .

"Don't I get a magic stone too?" Lars pushed against the stranger's knee, and again the pale flat eyes stared into his. "Why not me?"

"I gave you something more important than a lump of glass, boy. But if you can't see that for yourself, maybe I made the wrong choice."

"No. I mean . . . well, I don't understand, sir. What did you give me that you didn't give the others?"

"Power, me boy. Power!"

Lars stared. Then an excitement began to build up inside his chest, growing until he felt he would burst. Power!

He grabbed a stone, not even weighing it in his hand or checking its smoothness, and flicked it out across the water. Hop, hop, hop, hop . . . More hops even than the stranger had made. Why, it was true then. He could do *anything*.

The stranger smiled slowly. The smile started at the corners of his mouth and moved up his face, tilting his eyebrows and wrinkling the corners of his eyes. For an instant his flat pale eyes sparkled like night flies. "Now you understand," he said, but softly so that Lars alone could hear.

Then Grant came running back from the village, all out of breath, slipping on the rocks and scuffling against loose stones. "He wants to see you," he gasped, when he had his breath back. "President London. He's waiting for you in the dining hall. I'll show you the way."

"No." Lars stood up. "I will." He spoke so definitely that Grant just stood with his mouth open while the stranger climbed from his rock, shook out the folds of his cloak and walked towards the village with Lars at his side.

"It's not fair," Grant muttered. "After all I ran both ways."

"Never mind," said Marianne. "He did give us the magic

19

stones. Lars skipped *eight* hops and he wasn't even trying," she went on.

"Did he?" Grant stared after the two. "I don't think I like that man."

David N'Kumo was skinning purple-furs behind the kitchens when he heard voices. He looked up in time to see the red-and-gold stranger stride by with Lars Holmstrom. He stared and his knife went too deep and scored the soft skin. Bother! Mother would be angry if he'd spoiled it. She was saving purple-furs to make a bed coverlet for his sister Ruth, who was to be married after harvest.

He looked up again from the damage and found he was staring straight into the flat pale eyes of the stranger. They were fixed on the skins, but when he saw David staring at him he turned away and went on listening to Lars, who was chattering importantly.

" . . . no, Roger London is our *new* President. For years and years, oh long before I was born, it was his father Mark. But four winters ago That Old Woman took him, and they chose his son. Next year is election year. Then all the men get to decide if they want him to go on being President or if they'll pick someone else." Lars' voice faded as the two passed out of sight along the front of the kitchen towards the dining hall.

Who in the world was the stranger and where did he come from? David's skin prickled with curiosity. There were no other people on Isis, unless Uncle Jody's stories were to be believed. If so, there were but two, the Keeper and the Guardian. And they, according to Uncle Jody, lived alone at the place which men called World's End.

David finished skinning the purple-furs, left the skins furside down on the short turf and took the carcasses indoors. He hung them by their hind legs over one of the hooks in the larder at the end, the one that backed onto the dining room. It was the coolest store room, and fresh air

20

came in from a grating high in the wall.

He was just leaving when a voice floated down to him, small but clear.

"Michael Joseph Flynn, your honour. Come to pay me respects."

"But where are you *from*?" Roger London's voice was squeaky with panic. David grinned, remembering the old President, his height, his massive shoulders and beard, his deep voice and terrifying scowl. It was sometimes hard to believe that Roger was his eldest son.

"From the north." The stranger's words were casual, but they sent a shiver down David's spine. All of Isis was a mystery to the villagers, who were imprisoned in their own valley by the forbidden mountains; but the north was above all other places mysterious. The great storms came out of the north. In the north That Old Woman reigned over the kingdom of the dead . . . though that was all lies, Uncle Jody said, and he should know, since he was the only human to have set foot outside the valley since the Beginning Times.

"The . . . the north?" President London's voice stuttered with fear. "What do you want with us, sir?"

"Sure and to be your friend. And here's my hand on it. As to why I come, it is bearing gifts."

"Gifts? Why, you are from the Guardian, then? Are you . . . are you he?"

There was a silence. David, listening on the other side of the wall, was puzzled. Why would the stranger hesitate. If he *were* the Guardian he would surely know it.

"Sure and I am but a humble emissary," the stranger said at last.

"Huh?"

"A messenger. A messenger with gifts."

"From the Guardian! Well, well, we are fortunate indeed. Never before, never in all the years. There were the gifts, of course, indeed we are most appreciative of his gifts, sir. I hope you will tell him so. But a visit from . . . What was it

21

you said? An emissary. My goodness, yes. You will stay at my house of course. The best room. Anything you want you must ask for. Anything at all."

"Your kindness deserves reward. Allow me."

Another silence. David longed to know what it was that the stranger had given the President that had silenced his babblings so suddenly. He looked around the store room. There was a barrel of pickled fish in one corner. He pulled it quietly across the room until it was directly beneath the grating in the wall. He scrambled up. On tiptoe, with his fingers curled through the grating, he could just see down into the long dining hall.

The head table was directly below him on the other side of the wall. He could see the balding top of the President's head, and across from him, full face on, the stranger. Between them, passed from the stranger to the president, who held it in his right hand, was a stick of some whitish stuff, like nothing David had ever seen before.

"Thank you, sir. You are most good to your people."

"Sure and you're very welcome. But aren't you going to ask me what it is for?"

"A gift from the Guardian is a gift! It is not my place to ask what it is, any more than we asked of all your other gifts. The giving is enough."

An expression of annoyance flashed across the stranger's face; but it was gone so quickly that David wondered if he'd imagined it. "Sure and it is *your* place to ask. Are you not President of Isis? Lord of the planet?"

"Well . . ."

"Well, then, you must be a man of power. Why do you stare at me like that? Surely you'll not be denying the truth of me words?"

"Oh, no, sir. I would not think of it. It is only . . ." He stopped, and then began to speak quickly, but in such a low voice that David had to strain to catch the words. "I was *his* son, you know. All those years. He treated me like a child,

22

even when I was a husband and father. Contempt. That's what he felt for me, and he let me know it. Oh, yes. He never gave me a chance. It was always *him* first. Then when he died it was my turn at last. I thought it'd all be different. I thought everyone would accept me. That I'd feel important, that I'd be able to act the way he did, so that everyone would respect me. But it's not like that. Nothing's changed. Sometimes I feel that Father's still President, and still despising me, laughing at me." He gulped and then went on. "Next year is election year. And they won't pick me. I know they won't . . ." His voice died away in a mutter. David found himself feeling almost sorry for the poor fellow. He wondered if the stranger would laugh.

But Michael Flynn leaned across the table until his face was only a hand-span from the President's. "Roger London," he said in a low clear voice. "The gift I have given you is the answer to your wishes."

"This?" Roger held the stick limply between his finger and thumb.

"It is power, when you know how to use it. That is what you want, isn't it? Power."

The balding head nodded slowly. It lifted and the President stared at the stranger.

"Power. Yes. You *knew*. But how does it work?"

"I will show you."

David noticed that the stranger had dropped his foppish manners and his lilting accent. He spoke softly but firmly, as if he were somehow pressing the words into Roger London's mind.

"You must believe in power. It is in the wand. Hold it as if it were filled with power. Grasp it, man! Yes, that's better. Now you hold the Power you will sit straight, your shoulders square, your head up, your face serious. After all, to own Power is a serious matter, is it not? Ah, that is better. Now I will show you the kind of Power you possess."

From a satchel hidden in the folds of his cloak the stranger

23

drew a cup, ornately made, studded with coloured stones. He set it on the table between the two of them.

"See, it is empty. I will turn it upside down on the table. Now, President Roger London, strike it with your wand and remember your Power!"

David, his muscles cracking with the effort, stretched on tiptoe and saw the President's hand reach out and timidly tap the cup, as if he were afraid to break it.

Michael Flynn shook his head. "There was no Power in your mind or your hand." His voice was full of contempt, and David saw the President cringe. The stranger lifted the cup as if he had expected to see something beneath it, but of course there was nothing but the scrubbed surface of the table.

"Try again. Once more. If you fail I must look elsewhere. I have heard that among the younger men there is one that would be President."

"Jody N'Kumo. Never!" David was startled by the anger in the voice. It didn't even sound like Roger London's. The wand struck the cup and there came a mighty singing sound, very high and shrill, so you could hardly hear it, but it went through one like needles.

"Ah! The Power speaks." The stranger leaned back, a smile painted on his face. "Now lift the cup, President Roger London. Lift the cup!"

Roger London reached out with his left hand and slowly turned the cup over. He gasped and the cup slipped and rocked on its ornate base. On the other side of the wall David too let out a gasp. Then he ducked quickly down behind the grille, as the stranger's cold pale eyes flicked upward at the sound.

"That is Power," Michael Flynn whispered. David slowly straightened up until he could once more look down into the dining hall. There in the centre of the bare table lay a huge jewel, of the deepest blue he had ever seen, with fire burning in its heart. The light seemed to reach out to the shadowiest

24

corners of the room.

"Power." Roger London's hand crept forward towards the jewel.

Quickly the stranger upended the cup over it and the light was quenched. "Strike the cup again," he ordered, and when Roger London had obeyed him he lifted the cup. The table was bare, the room dark.

"But . . . it's gone!"

"The Power you released is now within the rod."

"Aah!"

"And in *you*, when you choose to use it," the stranger added very softly.

"Yes." Roger London's voice was a whisper too.

"So you have seen Power," the stranger went on matter-of-factly. "And now you believe in it, so will others." He stowed the cup away and from the same satchel brought out a small plain square box. He set it on the table and opened it briefly to show the President that it was empty.

"Now strike it with your wand, and think of food," he commanded. And when Roger London had obeyed him the front of the box fell open revealing a cube of some strange stuff.

"Well then, take it. Eat it. You'll not be thinking that I'm about to poison you?" He made to close the box as the President's hand hesitated.

"Wait. No. I'll . . . I'll try." The President broke off a small piece. There was a silence. He broke off another. Then the rest vanished into his mouth. "Mmmm. My goodness. It is delicious. Indescribable. What is it?"

"It is what *you* made with the Power. Now ask yourself: would you spend your days reaping and threshing and grinding and baking—or would you rather eat this?"

"You mean, you can make more?"

"I did not make it. *You* did. Yes, so long as there is Power in the wand you can make this food."

"No more work . . . and it is delicious. Simply delicious.

25

They will love it. All of them. They won't laugh. They're bound to re-elect me! Tell me, kind sir . . . does this substance have a name?"

The stranger paused. "Sure and I've always called it ambrosia. But you can please yourself."

"Ambrosia! Out of this little box! But I couldn't make enough of it to feed everyone, could I? Even if I worked at it all day."

"Sure and it's the great man you are to be thinking first of others! Enough for everyone, not just for yourself, is it? Well, I suppose it might be done. But you would still have to be in charge. Only you would have the Power."

"Yes, yes. Of course."

"We will talk about it later. But for now the Power is your secret. Yours and mine."

Again the President nodded. The stranger stood up and stretched. David climbed quietly down off the fish barrel and tiptoed towards the larder door. Roger London's voice floated down from the grating. "There must be something I can do for you in return for all these favours."

"Don't fret yourself, my friend. If I have any needs I'll be telling you. But for now, I have a curiosity to see around your settlement."

David ran down the passage. The kitchen aunties were at the sinks scrubbing vegetables and he got past them without being seen. He grabbed the purple-fur skins from the grass outside, and by the time President London and the stranger had strolled around the corner of the building he was beyond the village, his furs laid out on the smooth stones beside the river, scraping diligently away.

The stranger poked his nose into the kitchen and looked around with apparent interest. He pointed to the other door. "And what lies beyond there?"

"Larders, store rooms, that is all. Women's work."

But women's work or not, the stranger must have been interested, for he darted down the passage, opening each

26

door and poking his head inside. He stopped at the last room for so long that Roger London ambled after him to see what was so interesting.

There was nothing remarkable. The stone shelves where meat cut up for stew steeped in bowls of herbs. Skinned rock bunnies and purple-furs hanging from the ceiling hooks. A barrel of pickled fish against the wall. Nothing of interest. He said so.

The little man agreed and smiled. The smile did not reach his eyes, which were as opaque as stones. He looked up at the ventilation grille above the barrel, and the bloody palm print high up on the wall, as if someone with soiled hands had steadied himself against it. His smile widened.

He allowed himself to be shown the rest of the village, his eyes busy, his brain noting everything. He even noticed David, squatting by the skins, scraping away under the hot sun, his hands red with purple-fur blood.

Chapter Three

By supper time every person on Isis was talking about the stranger, and everyone had a different story about who he might be. David said nothing at all. After all, he had had no right to be in the larder, listening to the private conversation of the President.

In the dining hall the hubbub was amazing. Voices rose high and even quarrelsome. It was as if everyone had been changed into another kind of person. David wondered at it; why, on the way to supper he had had to separate two of the children who had come to blows over a coloured stone.

The President would put a stop to all the nonsense, once he appeared; he was a man who set great store by good manners. Only the President never came. Everyone sat politely waiting while dinner cooled in the big pots and the kitchen aunties grumbled.

At last the Council filed in and sat at the head table, and the Vice President mumbled grace and they could begin. Now everyone was quiet and people only whispered. Where was the President? It didn't seem like a proper meal with the head chair empty. And as for the stranger, what had become of him?

David caught his sister by her apron as she passed with a platter piled high with fresh bread. "Where's the President?" he hissed.

"Eating in his own house." Ruth's eyes were big at the

28

idea. "Can you believe it? He and the stranger eating alone. Bad manners I call it. I had to carry over a tray."

"Why should he do that? Is he ill?"

She shook her head. "I heard *him*—the stranger, you know—say that those with Power should keep apart from the rest. Power? Huh, what power, I ask you! It makes no sense at all."

She whisked away, leaving David to frown over his bowl of stew. He knew what Power was—a white wand that made jewels appear out of thin air and food in an empty box. But it still made no sense at all.

People were reluctant to leave the dining hall free for the youngers' supper. Surely the President and his guest would put in an appearance any time now. But twilight deepened and the bunnyfat lamps had to be lit. Outside the voices of the hungry children were high and querulous. Then came a voice, clearer than the rest.

"Look! Look in the sky above the Cascades. A moon, a new moon!"

The Vice President got to his feet and strode from the hall, the other members of the Council on his heels. Everyone crowded after them, anxious to see this new wonder. What a day it was being! The doorway jammed with people rudely pushing and jostling.

David picked up one of the big serving platters and carried it through to the kitchen as his excuse to use the back way.

"Well, wonders will never cease! Perhaps the young man is going to help us with the dishes also!" One of the aunties threw a towel at him, but he laughed and dodged her, and ran through the door to join the crowd outside.

Everyone was staring at the northern sky.

"That's no moon. The wind's got your brain," someone said. "Shu is passing yonder and Nut will not rise tonight until the Kettle is overhead. A child would know that."

"And a babe in arms would know that directly above the Cascades at this time and season is a patch of sky with only

29

six small stars that make a square that is called the Table," another voice retorted. "If you can count past six, then look. There *is* a new star. Or a new moon. Who can say which?"

"This has been a day of miracles," another said, and that ended the argument. A cool north wind sent the people shivering away, each to his own house.

David stared up at the the point of light shining where no light had ever shone before. The last vestige of twilight bleached out of the sky. As it darkened the stars grew brighter. Except for the new star. Its light grew fainter and fainter and soon he could no longer see it. A day of miracles indeed—a star that shone by day and not by night! He ran quickly home through the darkness.

As soon as the women and children returned from their meal Grandfather Isaac led the prayers, with the Bible open on the table in front of him. He didn't read it, though; he said that these days the small print bothered his old eyes. As for the younger ones, none of them knew how to read or cared much so long as there were memories to tell the stories.

David stared at the firelight and thought about the stranger and the Power, and wondered what it might mean. There was a prickly feeling in the air as if everything was changing.

"So we thank God for the abundant harvest," Grandfather's voice droned on, and David tried to pay attention. "And we pray Guardian to keep Isis safe in its place in the sky and Ra on its accustomed path around us so that we may have light and warmth by day and darkness for our sleep. We ask him to protect us from storms and keep us out of the clutches of That Old Woman."

Uncle Jody moved impatiently. David thought that Grandfather spoke of death as 'That Old Woman' purely to aggravate Jody. Often when prayers were over there would be a most unprayerful argument. But tonight it was little

Addie, of all people, who interrupted.

"The Guardian! Oh, Grandfather, people are saying that he is *here*. Himself. In the President's house!"

The young ones shivered pleasurably at the thought. It was one thing to pray to the Being who kept Isis in the sky and the seasons coming and going as they should. To have him actually staying in the village was something very strange.

"Nonsense," Uncle Jody exploded.

Nobody paid any attention. Uncle Jody was always saying 'nonsense'.

"Do you suppose it's really him?"

"They say that he works miracles!"

"Fiddle!"

"Uncle Jody, *that* at least is true." David could no longer contain his own particular piece of news. He told them what he'd seen. ". . . and then he produced food from an empty box and a jewel, all blue and lit from inside as if it were on fire . . ."

"He had a firestone?" Jody asked, suddenly intent.

"That's what it's called? You saw? Then you must believe he's Guardian."

"I didn't see what you saw. I've seen firestones before on Isis. *She* had many." He closed his mouth tightly as if he'd already said too much. David sighed. It was always so with Uncle Jody. It was as if he carried a burden of memory that could not be shared.

But then Uncle Jody *was* different. When only a boy he had been accused of breaking taboos and been banished from the valley, which had seemed to be a sentence of death, since it was known that no man could ever live on the heights or in the raging emptiness that must lie beyond the mountains at World's End.

Only Uncle Jody had not died. He had returned many many days later, his feet blistered but healing, his clothes in rags, but clean. He had given the lie to the old stories. Only no one would listen and now Jody was silent, while the old stories were passed on to youngers, like a comfortable pair of sandals already broken in to use.

"Bed," ordered Grandfather Isaac in the heavy silence that followed Jody's words. "Tomorrow the President is bound to speak to us. Or if not tomorrow then the next day. Meanwhile the harvest is ready and tomorrow we begin to reap. So go to bed, all of you, and no more nonsense about firestones and miracles. A man cannot fill his stomach with firestones or store them against winter."

Next morning the men and boys had breakfast in the dark and began to harvest the grain at first light. It was the best time of year, thought David, and the best time of day. Still cool enough to wear a shirt, and with a quiet not even interrupted by bird song. Just the swish of the scythe, the rustle of falling stalks, and the occasional scree-scree as a man stopped to sharpen his blade on his whetstone.

At first it was hard work, but after a while his muscles remembered the rhythm and he felt he could go on for ever. By the time Ra had climbed above the eastern mountains and the shadows had begun to shrink, the women and children were coming behind them, gathering the grain into bundles, tied with a twisted handgrasp of golden stalk. It was noisier now, with laughter from the youngers and gossip among the women as they moved steadily across the bright field.

David took off his shirt and worked in his breeches, his dark-skinned shoulders gleaming with sweat. To left and right of him the scythes moved in a rhythm of silver flashes and the golden stalks fell. Rockbunnies and purple-furs scampered from underfoot to hide in the uncut grass ahead.

He stretched for a minute, allowing a panic-sticken purple-fur time to escape, and looked back towards the shimmer of the lake. He longed for a drink and a wash. Ra was high now, almost overhead. It must be nearly lunchtime. He wiped his face with his hand and worked on.

At last there was a distant shout and a handwave, and the men laid down their scythes and walked slowly back through the silvery stubble. The kitchen aunties had pulled the tables out onto the grass in front of the dining hall. There were mounds of fresh bread, fruit, big circular cheeses and pitchers of cold water.

David paused by the river crossing to plunge his arms into the coldness and splash his sweating face. It was good to do a man's work, but hard and hot. As he walked towards the green he nearly fell over Marianne Oluk. She was crouched beside a rock, almost invisible in her brown home-spun gown and apron, and she was crying.

"What's the matter?"

"The boys are building a huge cage to put birds in. The stranger told them how and Lars is bossing them. I tried to stop them and he *hit* me."

"Well, I'll fix him if it'll make you feel better."

She shook her head and dried her eyes on the corner of her apron. "I don't care. But the poor little birds." She began to cry again.

"Don't cry. They'll never catch any. Birds are too fast and clever, you know that. And then you'll have the laugh on them, building a cage full of nothing!"

"But they *are* catching them. He showed Lars how, with sticky stuff. It's ever so cruel, David. I hate them!"

"Come on then." He took her hand and pulled her to her feet. "We'll go and break the silly cage and let the birds go, all right?"

"Oh, yes." She trotted beside him, two steps to each of his strides. But when they got to the green they were stopped by one of the Council and hissed at to sit on the grass and be quiet.

"Later," David whispered, and then forgot about the birds. A shiver of excitement ran through the crowd as President London strolled, in a very lordly way, across the green. Beside him, walking with a spritely dancing step, his sharp eyes darting from left to right, was the stranger.

The President hadn't done a hand's turn all morning, David noticed resentfully. In fact, in spite of the warmth, he had thrown a cloak over his shoulders, of patchwork design lined with purple-furs. David recognized it as a bedcover from the London household.

The stirrings and excited whispers grew and President London had to hold up his hand for silence.

"My people," he began pompously. "We have been blessed by a visit from an . . . an emissary of the Guardian himself. He has sent us this man, Michael Joseph Flynn, to show us a new way of living. Imagine never having to work for your food again. No more blistered hands or aching feet. He has shown me the secret of providing food in abundance for ever!"

The crowd roared and Roger London had to wave his hands agitatedly before he could be heard again. "Look, all of you, at this miracle." He took the white wand from his belt and struck a box that he placed on one of the tables among the platters of food. The side of the box fell open and within could be seen a cube of strange yellowish stuff.

"This is ambrosia," the president said in his squeaky voice, and he began to share it out as hands reached curiously towards the table. David was close enough to reach over and get a few crumbs. They tasted marvellous, melting in the mouth and leaving a flavour of fine nuts and honey, and a longing for more.

"More, we want more!" People around him were shouting, and David found himself shouting too. It just wasn't enough, that little taste. He craved another piece.

Meanwhile those further back who'd received none at all began to grumble. "That's not fair. We haven't had a morsel back here." And they began to push and shove.

"Wait, wait!" Roger London's voice trembled. He closed the box, struck it again, and again, when it opened, there was another cube of ambrosia. This time there was a fight to get a piece, and a child actually got knocked over and its hands trodden on before it was rescued.

"Please wait. There's enough for all." The President mopped at his forehead with a corner of his patchwork quilt, and looked frantically towards the stranger. *He* stood, it seemed, apart, with raised eyebrows and a faint amused smile on his face.

"There is more than enough," the President shrilled. "Even though the box is small the supply is endless. Only be patient!" He tapped the box once again, but when the side fell everyone could see that it was quite empty, not even a crumb inside.

The roars of the crowd turned to anger and Roger London's face grew pale. "I don't understand. Sir," he tugged at the stranger's cloak. "Look!"

As if he were only now aware of what had happened, the stranger started, frowned and examined the box. Then he closed it, waved his hands above it, muttering to himself, and then turned to Roger London. "Strike it now," he commanded. And when the President hit the box with his wand it fell open to disclose, not a cube of ambrosia, but a blue jewel with fire in its heart.

Everyone gasped in surprise. Everyone but David, who felt as if he were seeing a play that he had seen before. Only this stone, it seemed, was less brilliant than the other.

"Ahah!" The stranger picked up the stone, turning it around so that Ra's rays caught it and were returned as rays of fire. "The power comes from the stone, and alas, the stone is weakening. It is something in the air of this place. I apologize. I am sorry. My gift is worthless."

He shrugged, and picked up the box, turned away as if to leave. The President caught the corner of his cloak. "You can't leave now! You gave me the Power. You said it was mine. You must make it work again. You must!"

"Must?" The stranger's eyebrows went up. "No man says 'must' to Michael Flynn."

"I am sorry," the President gabbled. "I meant no discourtesy. Please stay. I beg you to stay. Anything you want. Anything." He gazed around and his shoulders sagged as he realised that Isis could have nothing to offer this man.

"Sure and aren't you kindness itself! I will stay then. But it grieves my heart not to be able to help you in return! If only I had more stones to replenish the Power, why then I could build you a box the size of that oven there, to supply you with ambrosia for ever. But alas, I found that stone on . . . at a place far far from here."

"I've seen that kind of stone before." A voice came from the crowd. "Stuck in the rock like fruit in a pudding."

"Have you really now? Well, well. That is an interesting concidence." The stranger smiled politely, but as if he were not really interested at all.

"Who spoke? Who was that?" Roger London stuck his head forward like an anxious turtle.

"It's Will Kovacs, President. I saw a stone like that in a lump of rock that fell off the mountain after the earth moved. It was right after Thanksgiving Day. Nine years ago, was it not? Or ten?"

"Aye, it was nine years all right."

"It was the year the river near flooded the village."

"Aye, and then the earth moved again and all was well."

"And where did the rock fall from?" the stranger asked, quite casually, as if it didn't matter. But David, who was standing a little in front of Will Kovacs, saw the stranger's eyes as he stared past him at Will. They were no longer flat and pale, but danced with light like a firestone.

"Over yonder," Will pointed towards the eastern rampart. "After the earth moved many big rocks tumbled down. We used them when we repaired the cemetery wall. In one of them was a stone like that one. Useless, but a pretty thing, I thought."

"Well, isn't that a piece of luck! If the stones hereabouts

36

have as much Power as those which I got in that other place, why, maybe I can help you build a Forever Machine after all. I will be giving a piece of ambrosia to every person who can find me an undamaged stone."

There was a rush through the village and up the slope to the cemetery. Food was trampled into the grass and cups were knocked over and smashed.

The cemetery was a peaceful place, kept free of thorn bushes and cactus, with neat rows of crosses made of bamboo. It was separated from the vegetable garden on one side and the mountain on the other by a low wall of red rock.

One of the youngers found the first stone. "There. In the wall. I can see it shine."

"No!" Uncle Jody stepped forward, but not fast enough. Those who had tasted ambrosia hungered for more. Those who had not were spurred on by the appetite of those who had. In a short span the neat wall was a scatter of boulders. Three blue stones with fire in their heart were found and chipped carefully from the surrounding rock, and taken triumphantly to the stranger.

But he 'tutted' and shook his head after he'd looked at them closely.

"What is the matter?"

"These are poor stones, feeble in comparison with mine." He held one up between finger and thumb. "Do you not see how the light refracts off the inclusions?"

The stones looked no different to the people, but they were impressed by the long words and looked at each other doubtfully.

"But that's all there were," someone said into the silence.

"Hmmm." The stranger looked up at the mountain, shading his eyes against the light. Beyond the blue-turfed hillock where the cemetery stood, a tongue of land rose up to connect with the red cliffs and jagged peaks that rimmed the valley.

"Up there. D'you see the dark line running across like meat in a sandwich? It is a vein of firestones, I'll stake my life on it. There'll be more than enough up there to power your Forever Machine."

"We cannot venture up there."

"It is taboo, stranger. Do you not know that?"

"Yes I know it. But what is done can be undone easily enough. What is forbidden can be permitted."

"That's true. After all he came from the Guardian."

"And the Guardian made the taboos."

Uncle Jody spoke, surprising David, and indeed everyone else. "You must know, stranger, that the oxygen is too thin for us to survive up there, and there is a danger from ultraviolet as well."

Nobody knew what Jody was talking about except the stranger. He stared, his face suddenly confused, and Jody stared grimly back. It was as if in the exchange of these strange words 'oxygen' and 'ultra-violet' that the two had recognized that they were enemies who shared the same secret.

There was a chorus of objections. "It's only Jody N'Kumo."

"Spouting nonsense again!"

The stranger smiled and raised his hand. The voices quietened. "I will bring you a message from the Guardian." There was a gasp. "Yes, he himself will tell you what he wants you to do. Will you do as he says?"

"Aye."

"Of course, sir."

"The Guardian speaking to *us*!"

The stranger nodded and stalked away down the slope. David saw him call Lars Holmstrom and walk along with him, talking rapidly, one arm draped carelessly over the boy's shoulder. What could he be saying to Lars? One of the youngers. David was about to run down the slope after them when Uncle Jody caught his arm.

"Come, David. Help me rebuild the wall."

"Can't it wait? *They're* not going anywhere." The crude joke slipped out before he could stop it. How could he think such a thing? He flushed and bent down to hoist a heavy stone back into place.

Uncle Jody worked silently beside him, his dark brows drawn together into a frown, his lower lip protruding. He looked angry, obstinate and puzzled.

"D'you know where the N'Kumo family came from?" he asked suddenly.

"Came from? Where else but this valley."

"I mean in the Before Times."

"From Earth?" David smiled. The legend that the people of Isis had sailed from a star called Earth in a winged ship called Pegasus was still told every Thanksgiving.

"It is true. Don't laugh at it, David. My own grandfather came from Earth as a small boy. From a place called East Africa. And do you know what the N'Kumos were in Africa?"

David shook his head.

"They were men. They were lion-killers. They were not greedy children chasing firestones."

"But it is not the stones, it is the Power, Uncle Jody. Imagine having food like that every day of your life without having to lift a finger."

"Fiddle. I do not believe any of the stories of Michael Joseph Flynn. I know he did not come from Guardian. I do not believe he even came from Isis!"

"How could he come from anywhere else? Where else is there?"

"There is space. He could have come through space from another planet. A place like Earth. It is possible."

David was just about to contradict his uncle when he remembered the golden bird that he had seen land on the top of Lighthouse Mesa. He stopped with his mouth open.

"What is it?"

David explained. "Could it have come from another place?"

39

"Perhaps. I think so."

"But that doesn't mean he's bad. After all, he wants to help us by making the Forever Machine."

"How kind of him! But why?"

"If the Guardian sent him . . ."

"No! Of that I am absolutely certain, Jody."

"The President will never believe you. He likes the stranger."

"Of course. The man gives him what he most wants."

"Then there's no good talking about it, is there?"

Uncle Jody sighed and straightened. "You're right. No one will believe me. Nothing has changed."

He stopped to fit a big stone into a corner of the wall. David worked on. Uncle Jody was right and all the others were wrong. He felt it in his bones, and not just because he was his uncle. But how much easier it would be to be like the others. To believe the stranger and do whatever he asked. After all, maybe it was intended for the best. Why should the stranger wish them ill?

He looked down across the valley and beyond the lake to where the silver stubble stretched to the wavery line where they had stopped cutting the grain that morning. The scythe blades caught the sun. How extraordinary that everyone should be standing around talking instead of going back to work. After all, before long the winds would come, sweeping out of the north and flattening any grain that had not been harvested. They should be working now, while the weather was good.

Uncle Jody followed his gaze. "Come on," he said grimly. "Perhaps you and I can bring them to their senses."

They crossed the river and picked up their scythes. The others laughed at them.

"Who needs to sweat?"

"We'll get everything we need without all this work, and better tasting too."

But a few men joined Jody and David, and a few of the

40

women came behind to bind and stook. Only a very few. By the time Ra slid behind the western mountains they had made only a small dent, like a bite out of a slice of bread, in the line that stretched clear across the valley.

"How much longer?" David wiped his forehead with his arm.

"Until we can no longer see," Uncle Jody answered.

David grinned tiredly. "All right, lion-killer."

Jody looked across the lake towards the village. "No lion there," he said softly. "More like a jackal."

Chapter Four

The second flyer dropped from its pod and fell towards Isis. The braking jets flared and Moira banked expertly and spiralled down towards the rift valley system. She could see now that it stretched for many hundreds of kilometres north and south, and consisted of two river systems springing from a single mountain range to flow in opposite directions.

Where was Mike? There was no hint in the rugged landscape to tell her that one place was more likely than another. I'll start in the north and work my way south, Moira told herself. An enormously long wide valley made an excellent landing strip and she coasted in, coming to a halt in the shadow of southern mountains.

Behind her a plume of red dust trailed and fell softly back to the ground. She unlocked the canopy and pushed it open. She breathed sweet thin air, and listened.

There was the sound of water falling close at hand. A thin rustle of papery leaves. A gust of wind from the north lifted her hair; she could hear it talking in the high grass and rattling dry branches together. In the distance there was a random sound like the tapping of tribal drums.

Then there were people here, though she could see no one. Primitive agricultural . . . and drums . . . Suppose they killed and ate strangers? Some did. Suppose . . . ?

"MIKE!" she stood up in the flyer and yelled as loudly as she could.

Bong. Bong. The drum sound came again. She scrambled out and jumped from wing to ground. Bong-bong. Bong-bong-bong. Where? What? Her eyes scanned the long grass, the sparse thorn bushes, the dry turf that ran up to the naked mountains. Nothing moved but the wind through the grass and the thorn bushes. Bong.

The wind dropped and the planet waited in silence. The drum sound stopped too, to resume as soon as the wind blew once more, touching the tall grey trees up on the hill to her left. They were not trees at all, she suddenly realised, but a species of incredibly tall bamboo. When the wind passed between them they swayed gently and touched each other, ringing with a hollow drum-like noise.

Her hand relaxed from the laser and she looked around fearlessly. Beyond the grove the short upland turf ran blue to the stony red feet of the mountain cliff to her left. From it an escarpment swooped low to join one from the mountains to her right. It was as if two giants grasped hands to form a bridge. It was from this scarp that she could hear water falling.

She walked around the flyer, waist deep in dry grass heavy with red seed-heads, to discover a river. She followed it upstream to a little glen, crowded with flowers and low bushes, lush and green under the spray of the waterfall. Quiet and empty.

Then her heart pounded and fear prickled her skin, for, standing in the shadows, his back towards her, was a giant of a man. Was it possible that he hadn't heard the flyer? That he hadn't turned from his contemplation of the falling water to see it land? That he wasn't even interested?

Moira walked cautiously forward. Still he didn't move.

"Hello, there!" She spoke in English and again in Intergalactic. Was the man deaf?

The westering sun caught the smooth top of his head and for an instant it flamed silver-gold, blinding her. With a different kind of shock she realised that he was only a statue. She giggled

43

in relief and wiped her suddenly sweaty palms on the legs of her jumpsuit.

How beautiful he was, perfectly proportioned; and the unknown sculptor had given the face a serene nobility. He looked wise and remotely sad, the eyes of clouded crystal gazing across the pool at the smooth bush-shrouded rock face beside the waterfall.

"You're beautiful. I wonder who made you—and why. You . . . you don't *belong* here."

Moira shivered suddenly and turned back to the flyer. There was no one here. She must head south if she was to find Mike.

"Olwen, is that you?" A voice spoke behind her, creaky, disused, like a rusty gate.

She whirled around, her heart pounding. But there was no one there.

"Who spoke? Where are you?" Her voice ran up the scale into a squeak.

Was it possible for someone to be hidden in the bushes that crowded the scarp below the waterfall? Watching her? A tremor of movement caught her eye, blurred and out of focus.

She blinked and stared. The gold head moved. The crystal eyes now gleamed, alive. The statue spoke.

"*You* are not Olwen. You are *not* Olwen!"

How could a robot voice hold so much sorrow, so much passion? Fear was replaced with pity. Pity? For a robot? She must be going out of her mind!

She walked back into the glade and faced the figure towering above her. "I am Moira Flynn. Who are you?"

"I am DaCoP 43. I was once the Guardian."

"Of all this?" Moira waved her hand to encompass the valley, the enclosing mountains, the distant horizon.

"No. The Guardian of Olwen." Again the note of sorrow.

"Where is she?"

The robot did not answer her directly, but walked stiffly, as if walking were an art that it had almost forgotten,

44

towards the rock wall at the back of the glade. It was masked shoulder-high in flowering bushes, but when the robot had pushed these to one side Moira could see than an area had been smoothed and laser-cut with an inscription:

OLWEN PENDENNIS
THE KEEPER OF THE ISIS LIGHT
Born 2064 Earth Orbit
Died 2149
'Where you go I may not follow'

The spray from the falls gleamed darkly on the rock and a faint green slime clung to the incisions.

" 'Where you go I may not follow'. How sad that sounds! What does it mean?"

"She was my friend. She made me . . . almost alive. I would have been happy to have died with her."

"But robots cannot die, not really."

"That is correct. I buried her here. It was her favourite place in the valley. It is beautiful, is it not? When I had finished the inscription on the rock, I switched myself off."

"A kind of death?"

"Yes. But not with her. A . . . a nothingness. How long have I been away?"

"It's now the year 2152 by Earth Orbiting reckoning." She glanced again at the inscription on the rock. "You've been switched off for three years!"

"Is that all? I wonder why I came back. It must have been your voice. It is like hers, with a lilt to it. You do not look like her, and her hair was red, not black. But you have some of the same grace."

Moira found herself blushing—at the compliments of a robot? She'd better get herself to some civilised planet before her brain turned to mush entirely! But he was questioning her now . . .

"But you cannot be from the colony! Your clothes . . . and you have a laser gun, a flyer." His voice changed. He was no longer to be pitied. He had become an avenging giant with fiery eyes and God knows what secret weapons about his person. "Why are you here?" he thundered.

Moira backed slowly away, talking as quickly as she could, explaining about the damage to the hyperdrive, and then, with more difficulty, about Mike's little ways on strange planets.

". . . and I'm really sorry about breaking quarantine," she concluded. "All I want to do is to get him back on board and away before he tricks these innocent folks out of their shoes and breeches."

"He can do that? How?"

"Oh, he has a silver tongue and speech like honey and a mind that's quicker than a bird's flight. Add to that he's the most awful liar in God's Galaxy, and the worst of it is he believes every word he's saying while he's saying it, even the most terrible rubbish. That's his secret. He believes himself."

"You love him, don't you?"

Moira sighed. "Yes, I suppose I do. I must, mustn't I? Or why would I put up with his nonsense all these years?" She felt a sudden longing to confide in this golden figure, to lay her head against his metal chest and have a good long cry. I must be going out of my mind entirely, she thought despairingly. Perhaps it's the altitude. I need another oxygen tablet to get me poor wits back.

She spoke stiffly, not to show her feelings. "If you will just tell me where the people on Isis live, for that's where I'll find my Dad, then I'll be off and trouble you no more."

"No trouble." The robot spoke absently. "How long has he been alone down here?"

"Three weeks."

"If he is the sort of man you say, he could already have caused much mischief. Why did you wait so long?"

"I was repairing the hyperdrive. It was only when I went to call him, when I'd finished, that I found out what he'd done to the radio. So I wouldn't hear your signal. I suppose it *was* yours? So that I wouldn't know straight away that he'd broken the rules again . . ." Her voice trailed off. It was always the same. Trying to explain Mike made her whole life seem so dingy and second-rate.

She swallowed and went on. "You've got to understand." Why was it important to explain Mike to this golden robot? "Mike's not little or mean. He has big ideas, great ideas! And the imagination in him—you wouldn't credit. But that's the trouble. He gets a truly great notion in his head and then he can't be bothered with anything that gets in the way of it. He sort of, well, pushes other things to the side."

"I understand. I'll help you all I can. We'll get your father out of here."

Moira cheered up and blew her nose and washed her face in the icy water of the pool. "Oh, thank you! They'll listen to you, I'll be bound, so powerful and gold and gorgeous looking. And they'll toss Mike out on your say-so. Why, they must believe that you're nothing less than a god!"

"You are right. And that is why I must not interfere if it can be helped."

Her smile faded. "But you said . . . Oh, Guardian, you can pick him up out of whatever mischief he's in as quickly and neatly as picking a snail out of its shell. Then we'll be off and away and we'll trouble you no more, I swear it!"

"I am sorry, but my mistress bound me with a promise that is stronger than all your words, Moira. I must not interfere, unless it is a matter of life and death. No one in Cascade Valley, which is the settlers' home, knows that I exist. Only in story and legend, and that is fading fast from their memories. Yes, you are right. They would think that I was a god. It happened before and it must not happen again."

"I could explain. I could tell them that you were only a robot. I hope I'm not offending you?"

"Not at all. It is an accurate statement of my being. But you are not being logical. The idea of a robot would be every bit as marvellous and magical to them."

47

"Then what in heaven's name *can* we do?"

"I think the best plan would be for both of us to fly down to Cascade Valley. I have a small floater that is quieter and more inconspicuous than your flyer. Once we are there I shall remain in hiding, while you go down into the valley and find out what your father is doing. After all, it is possible that he will already be ready to leave, with a little persuasion."

Moira shook her head and sighed. "He's been down here all of three weeks. It must be a great caper he's got going, a real beauty. Getting him away from it will be like prying a leech off a beefsteak tree. The only persuasion he's ever paid attention to has been the planetary police. I suppose you don't have . . ? No, I was afraid not. Oh, dear."

"Waiting will make the situation worse. I suggest we leave at once." The Guardian's eyes glowed. He looked livelier every minute.

"You've thought of a plan, haven't you?"

"Any number of them. But it is time-wasting to discuss them until we know the facts. Come. My floater is over here."

He stalked through the grove of giant bamboos. Moira, trying to keep up with his long legs, was running and quite out of breath when he stopped by a small old-fashioned floater, entirely covered with red dust.

Guardian tutted and brushed it away. "I should have covered it. We have occasional bad storms on Isis that bring dust from the great desert that lies beyond the northern mountains. I cannot understand why I forgot to cover it."

"You must have had other things on your mind," said Moira gently, remembering the grave beside the waterfall.

"That is true. But it should not have happened. I hope the floater is still functioning adequately." He climbed in, raising a cloud of dust as he settled himself. He turned a switch. There was a hum that became a high-pitched whine. It lasted for an unbearable ten seconds while Moira covered

48

her ears. There was a blue flash, a sharp crack and a small thread of smoke. Then silence.

"I should definitely have covered it." This failure of normal procedure seemed to have disoriented the robot. He continued to sit in the useless floater, shaking his head slowly from side to side.

Moira felt sorry for him. "Well now, it's a shame, no doubt about it. But there's no real harm done, Guardian, and there's no use in sitting crying over sand-blasted engines, is there? We'll have to go in my flyer, that's all. It may be larger and noisier, but we've no choice in the matter."

She persuaded Guardian out of his floater and back down through the grove. Close by the pool he baulked for a moment. But she took his hand and pulled it. "Later," she told him gently. "Nothing'll change here, will it now? You can come back to her later."

Once inside the flyer the unfamiliar surroundings seemed to arouse him. He looked eagerly around, his crystal eyes flashing. "My goodness," he said at last, "things *have* changed. Is it like this all over the Galaxy?"

"Oh, no. There's plenty better. This old crate is twenty years out of date. But we've patched it and added to it, a bit of this and a piece of that from every Tech planet we've ever touched at. Mike has always been a grand man for scrounging. Though of course there are many planets like Isis that are all agricultural. Why, on some machinery is actually a crime. The Galaxy's a real mixture now. And at every planetfall you get a different kind."

"You enjoy travel?"

"To tell you the truth there's nothing I'd like better than to settle down on a quiet little planet—something like this one would be grand—and never move farther than I could see from my own hearth."

"Then why do you go on travelling?"

She sighed. "I must, so long as Mike's got itchy feet, and

he'll have them till the day they bury him, I'm afraid. I promised my Mam, you see . . ."

"Well, don't cry about it. Show me how this flyer works."

Moira sniffed and then laughed. She'd been helping him, and now here he was cheering her. "Strap yourself in then and watch the video screen. I'm to head south, I suppose?"

The sun, small, hot and white in the blue-green sky, was still above the horizon when Guardian leaned forward and pointed at the screen with one long metal finger. "There. See that flat col between the two mountain ranges ahead. Come in low, Moira, so that we cannot be seen from the valley beyond."

She nodded and glided in smoothly, bringing the flyer to a whispering halt that barely disturbed the loose stones that littered the col. A glance at the atmosphere indicator told her that the oxygen outside would be low, but not dangerously so, if she remembered to take a pill every now and then to increase the effectiveness of her haemoglobin. She took one now, and slipped a bottle of them into her breast pocket.

Her personal force field belt would take care of the ultra-violet. There was plenty of water, and since the people were from Earth, what they ate she could eat. Wild beasts? Or wild people? She'd had to protect herself from both on many a planetfall. She picked up her laser and felt Guardian's hand on her wrist with a pressure which made her gasp and drop the gun.

"Why? You must know I'd only use it if I had to. And never to kill. Only to stun."

"You must not take any of your technology down into the valley. They're not ready for it. They don't yet have that kind of wisdom."

"Mike will have taken all kinds of gadgets, you know. He's already spoiled their . . . their innocence."

"Nevertheless I do not wish you to, Moira."

"I've got to fight fire with fire, Guardian."

"If you fight evil with evil there will be no winners—only victims."

She sighed. "What am I going to do?"

"Use your wits, girl."

"Against the wittiest man who has ever conned his way round the Galaxy?"

"You're his daughter. You must know how he thinks."

"I suppose I've picked up a trick or two. But I'll never surprise him. Well, all right. But I must take my force field."

"What does it look like?"

She showed him the jewelled belt around her waist.

"It is a beautiful ornament. But be careful. Let no one know of its powers."

"I'll be careful. So how do I look?" She shook her hair free of the knot she had tucked it into for flying. A small slim figure in a silver jumpsuit, unadorned except for the belt around her waist and the wide band that circled her left wrist. She waited for his inspection.

"That is a communicator?" He touched the bracelet.

"Yes. Three band. One to the ship. One between the flyers. And one directly to Mike. Only he's not talking nor listening either, I'd guess."

"So you and I can keep in touch?"

"Yes. I'll show you how. Perhaps we should set up a daily time."

"I will remain in the flyer during the nights. I require no sleep, of course, but I would like to read and study the mechanisms on board. During the day I must spend some time in the sun to replenish my energy cells. But we could set up a time during the day if you wish."

"No. We'll stick to night. But I still don't know what I'm actually going to do, if Mike refuses to come with me."

"There is a family that will help you, and one man especially. Jody N'Kumo, remember that name, the young one, not the grandfather. Tell him everything and ask for his help. He alone knows about me and Olwen. He alone

51

understands the truth about Isis."

Before she could ask 'what truth?' he climbed out of the flyer and stalked off towards the lip of the col. Here she found him looking down into a pretty valley. It had none of the fairytale beauty of the valley where Olwen was buried, but it was charming in a domestic sort of way.

Directly below the col the water fell in a series of cascades into a deep pool, worn ever deeper by the constant pounding of the water on the rock. Then it foamed and fussed down a narrow valley bounded on both sides by ramparts of red rock, and on the right also by an odd plug of rock almost as high as the surrounding mountains, flat-topped, sheer-sided, like the *mesas* on Earth, or the *lyors* of Northern Denebon Five.

Beyond the mesa the mountains drew back and the valley widened into a huge almost circular plain, rimmed like a bowl by cliffs and peaks. The river spread into a shimmering lake and then meandered through a reedy swamp before plunging through an archway set in a high circular wall. Within this enclosure it seemed to vanish.

Moira pointed. "Where does it go?"

"Down a volcanic vent. It flows underground until it is forced up into the mountains far beyond this valley."

"Why the wall?"

"Originally it was built to protect the early settlers from the vent holes—the ground is riddled with them down there. It was once taboo—it may still be."

Moira nodded and filed away the information in her mind. Every planet had its own quirks, its own taboos. When you were a Galactic wanderer you learned to go along with them, however odd they might seem.

She looked down at the village. The houses lay in neat rows between the shore of the lake and the foothills to her left. They were an odd mixture of early Tech plastic foam, and bamboo tied together with vines. There were fishing boats moored below the village, and across the lake rows of trees, heavy with fruit, were mirrored in the still water. Beyond the orchards, reaching out westward across the good bottom land, were squares of cultivation. Beyond them the wide valley shimmered with red grass.

It was a charming, domestic scene, a picture for a calendar or a jigsaw puzzle. But the place seemed to be deserted. Was it a holiday?

Guardian echoed her worries. "Something is wrong. There has been no storm warning, so they are not in the cave. It is harvest time and the fields have hardly been touched. Fish rise in the evening and no one is fishing. Something has gone terribly wrong!"

Chapter Five

"Something has gone terribly wrong," Guardian had said. Moira's heart thumped as she picked her way carefully along the stony river bank towards the strange village. Mike, she thought. What have you done this time? What awful trouble are you in and how am I to get you out of it?

Suddenly she was out of the shadow of the narrow valley, blinking in a flood of gold evening light. The village seemed deserted. Beyond the silent lake, where the reflections were broken occasionally by the circular ripples of rising fish, she could see the abandoned harvest.

Now the rocky valley walls to her left drew back and she could see the circular sweep of the enclosing mountains. Now she knew where the people were; the eastern rim of the valley seethed with activity like a broken ant hill.

Cautiously she back-tracked to the shadow of a rock and climbed up to a place where she could watch without being seen. There were a dozen ladders, leading up the almost vertical cliff face to a narrow platform made of bamboo lengths lashed together with rope. Along the platform as many as a hundred men laboured, pounding at the rock with crude hammers.

One of the men turned and for a second she saw his face clearly. It was dust red, but lines of sweat had marked furrows of grey in it. Grooves of fatigue or pain, she couldn't tell which, ran from nose to mouth.

54

They all moved with a painful slowness, as if they had forgotten the joy of being alive. The only break in the constant hammering came when a basket, filled with pieces of red rock, was passed along the line to one of the ladders, to be handed down, shoulder to shoulder, to the ground.

Sitting on the blue turf below the cliff, another gang of workers broke apart the rock lumps and picked at the pieces with knives and fingers. Around them mounds of broken rock stained the blue turf. Nobody stopped to talk or rest. All worked on at a dogged sad pace. Isis' sun dropped slowly towards the western mountains and in its brilliance the shadows of the workers made slow-moving patches of black against the red.

Moira lay on her rocky outcrop while tears welled up hot and ashamed and fell on her forearms and on the alien red soil. At last she slid down, blew her nose and washed her face in the icy water of the river and set off towards the village as fast as she could walk. She couldn't wait to find Mike and drag him away from this pretty little planet before he spoiled it and everything on it.

Where would he be found? Not up among the workers, no, not Michael Joseph Flynn, with his fine clothes and his honeyed words, himself descended from the ancient kings of Ireland, or so he would tell anyone who would listen. Not in any of the little bamboo shacks either, she would guess. Towards the centre of the village, close to the lake, there were houses built of plastic foam, old now and a little dingy perhaps, but a last remains of Earth technology on Isis.

The very biggest house would be the dining hall and meeting place, she guessed, and the long block house close by would be the washrooms. West of these, facing directly on the lake, was a house that seemed more important than the others. She walked right up to it and knocked boldly on the door.

It was opened by a middle-aged woman, plump and cross. "Who in the world would be knocking while I'm about to serve dinner to his . . . OH!" Her complaint turned into a scream as Moira stepped back from the shadowy doorway and became visible in the last rays of the sun.

"I'm wishing to see your visitor," Moira bluffed and stepped forward again, forcing herself in as the woman began to close the door against her.

She found herself in a large room with a fireplace, table and benches, a couple of rough chests against the wall, and two imposing chairs drawn up by the fire. The table was laid for two. In one of the chairs sprawled a familiar figure.

"Michael Joseph Flynn!"

He stirred lazily and looked up at her. "Me darling daughter!" His eyebrows went up at a pixy angle and his thin lips quirked into a smile. He raised the goblet he held in his right hand. "Sure and it's a pleasure to see your lovely face again. Sit down and have a sip of the smoothest wine this side of the galaxy. A delicious wine, but over mild. I've a mind to teach them the way of making brandy from the same berry. What a gift that would be for them! But there's little enough time, probably be wasted on them. They're a dull lot. But sit down, girl, sit."

"I will not sit. And I will not drink your wine. Little enough time, is it? There is no time at all. The drive is mended and we must be off today."

"Today? Oh, that's entirely impossible, dear girl. You don't know what you're asking."

"It's staying here that's impossible. Oh, Dad, what's your game? You must have known that I'd fix the radio and find out about the quarantine. How *could* you?"

"Quarantine?" His pale eyes widened. "What are you about now? And the radio? That broken too? No wonder you never got my messages."

"Mike Flynn, don't play your games with me. I know you took the second-stage condenser. And you knew about the quarantine. You read about it in Blackie's *Planets*. What else is there about Isis that you didn't want me to read?

56

What's your caper this time, Dad?"

"Caper, is it? What a wicked way to speak to your own father. Sit down or you'll not get another word out of me. You're giving me a stiff neck standing over me like some blessed police guard."

With a sigh Moira perched on the end of one of the benches. "Go on then. Tell me the truth, Father, or so help me it'll be the last time, I swear. As soon as we hit a civilized planet I'll leave you. I'll settle down and lead a normal life like an ordinary girl. Get a job and earn honest money for a change. Maybe even get married and raise a family. I swear I'll leave you, Mike Flynn, if you don't tell me the whole truth right this minute with no wool on it!"

"You'd never leave your old Dad," he said confidently. "But I'll tell you anyway to show I've no hard feelings for your disrespect." He sprang lightly to his feet and danced around the room. "And to tell the truth, it's a pleasure to share it, for it's a lovely plan! And when it's wound up we'll be rich, richer than you could ever imagine. We'll not have to wander the Galaxy, we'll settle wherever you point your finger, I promise. And I'll build you a house fit for a queen, furnished with all the treasures of the Galaxy."

"And where would these riches be coming from, if I may be so bold?"

"From these." He drew from his side pocket a handful of stones, a skyful of stars and suns that sent ruby lights quivering into the dark corners of the room.

"Firestones? Mike! Where did you get them? Why, they are the most . . . Where?"

"*Here.* Would you believe it? *The Luck of the Irish* threw us out of hyperspace to orbit the one planet in the entire Galaxy where they've found beauties like these. And the jest of it is that the poor fools living here haven't the least notion what they're worth. The stones are mine for the taking, and I've even got them to do the digging for me, so I won't blister me poor hands in the work. Isn't that the joke?"

57

"Sure and it's a great joke to con a couple of hundred innocent people into doing your dirty work for you."

"Couple of hundred is it? Why, that's but the one shift. I've four times that number working every living hour of daylight. It's a crying shame they've no electricity, otherwise I could have them going round the clock."

"I hope you're paying them well, Dad."

"Payment is it?" He chuckled. "Sure and I'm doing better than mere money. I'm giving them what every man dreams of. Power and the promise of a free ride through life."

"Oh, Mike Flynn, you're a bastard! I knew it was nothing but a caper. And what put you onto firestones in the first place?"

"I picked up two of them in a poker game on Wallania, I think it was. I've had them by me since then, sewn in me cloak for a rainy day. A lovely rainy day. And there it was, right in Blackie's *Planets*. The original exploration team found them on Isis and swopped them with goods from passing freighters—that was before the quarantine, of course. When I read those words I remembered the stones in me cloak and I said: Mike Flynn, your day has finally come. It is your guardian angel has brought you here and that's God's truth!"

"Well, your guardian angel's taking you off here and sharp, mind you that. We're off, Mike, this minute!"

"Listen to her then! And how are you going to make me leave before I'm good and ready?"

"I . . ." Moira hesitated. On other planets where Mike had got into trouble the people or the police, or both, had been only to eager to help her remove Mike. Her only trouble was to get him back in one piece, not skinned or dismembered. "I'll tell the President what you're up to," she bluffed. "That you're going to take the firestones and leave them nothing."

"Nothing? I'm leaving them a Forever Machine."

"And what in the name of heaven is *that*?"

58

"It's a lovely name, is it not? Has a ring to it. One of my best ideas, though I say it myself."

"Mike!"

"It's powered by firestones, so they think, and it'll deliver them a lifetime supply of ambrosia."

"Huh?"

"Honeycake from Quateb, remember?"

"Oh, I remember *that* all right. And that it's illegal to take the filthy stuff off the planet. How did you smuggle it out? No, I don't think I want to know. But how is your Forever Machine going to produce a lifetime's supply of an illegal drug made on a planet twelve parsecs from here?"

"It won't, you silly child. I wouldn't do that. It'd be bad for them. They might finish up addicted. No, all they'll get is one more taste, just to hold them till we're back up in *The Luck of the Irish*."

"Together with all the firestones they've mined."

"That's it, me clever girl. Isn't it lovely? And not a thing to go wrong."

Moira sighed. "Oh, it's a lovely plan, I grant you, Dad. But can you not see that it's *wrong*. They're innocents, these people. And you've no right to use them like slaves, exhausted and neglecting their harvest. What will they be eating next winter when we've gone and they've nothing but empty promises in the larder? I'm ashamed of you and that's the truth of it."

"Three hours a day and she calls it slavery? You're getting soft, Moira."

"Mike, listen. It's killing them. They're not able to bear the altitude or the ultra-violet. Have you thought about skin cancer? Oh, Dad, have you thought at all!"

He sulked, poured himself another goblet of wine and slumped in the chair by the fire. "Sure and you're an ungrateful girl, when it's all for you that I'm toiling."

"I don't want it, Dad. I won't touch it. Do you hear me?" She stood over him, hands on hips, cheeks burning with anger. Behind her a door shut.

"You certainly won't." Mike's voice changed, to become crisp and loud. "Lay a hand on the firestones or the Forever Machine and these people will throw you out of their valley!"

"Huh?" Moira stared. Mike was sitting up now, his eyes grey and opaque, his lips grim, the picture of outrage.

"Who is this stranger?"

She whirled to confront a pudgy man standing in the doorway. He was dressed in brown homespun, but wore around his shoulders an antique patchwork quilt, with an air that was obviously intended to be regal, but was merely pompous. She turned away.

"Come on then, Mike. Let's leave these people in peace. Keep what's already in your pocket, since it's little use to them, and let's be off before there's any more harm done."

"You can't leave now!" The pudgy man's voice was high and alarmed.

Mike raised an eyebrow to Moira, as if to say: you see? Then he addressed the villager. "President London, I must warn you that this woman is evil. She wants to destroy everything I have come here to do. She . . ."

"That's not true! I've come here to help you."

"She wants to stop your people digging for firestones. She wants to stop me building the Forever Machine. She would even prevent you eating ambrosia."

"It's not like that. He's twisting it all. I'm his daughter, and I . . ."

"She claims to be my daughter," Mike interrupted smoothly. "Though you know no daughter would speak to her father as she has spoken to me. She has come from the north and you should send her back there."

President London's pudgy face grew even paler. "Then is she also from the Guardian?"

"You ask that when I've told you she wants only to destroy my work?"

60

"Preserve us, she is from That Old Woman." His face was as pale as a moon, and he sank limply to a chair.

"Now you've done it, Dad," muttered Moira under her breath. "You and your foolish lies."

Her father ignored her and went to stand by President London. "She is not That Old Woman," he said soothingly. "The north is full of mischievous spirits, and she is only one of these. Like a stinging fly, a nuisance, but of no importance."

"Then we can send her away?"

"Do, my dear sir."

"Mike!" Moira appealed to him, but he looked through her as if she wasn't even there. She bit her lip. After all, he was only play-acting, the way he did.

The President shouted and knocked on the other doors of the house, rousing sleepy young men, tousled and half-dressed. At his order she was pulled from the house. One man's hands were viciously hard on her arms and she managed to bite him. But there were too many of them and she soon stopped struggling.

"Now what shall we do with her, sir?"

"A week in jail would do fine."

The men stared. "Jail? We do not understand."

"Oh sure and it's a helpless bunch you are . . ." Mike stopped, took a breath and smiled. "Tell me what you do with people that break your laws."

Roger London's face shone pale in the twilight. "There is no punishment but banishment from the Valley, and that has happened only once in our history. Little disagreements are settled before the Council. Do you think . . ."

"This is no little disagreement." Mike frowned fiercely. "The woman wants to destroy everything I've promised you. You had better banish her."

"I suppose you are right. Oh, dear." The fat hands twisted together while he made up his mind. "Take her up to the Cascades, boys, and make sure she leaves and doesn't come back."

61

"Better mount a guard," Mike suggested.

"But . . ."

"Tomorrow we begin to assemble the Forever Machine," Mike promised. "She mustn't interfere. Come, you've four hundred able men here."

"Not any more. Many are sick with the mountain sickness. Every man and woman left is already working. Why, you even had me remove the guard from the Sacred Cave, which has never been done before in the history of Isis."

A frown shadowed Mike's face. He sulked. Then, like a cloud leaving the sun, his face was cheerful again and he smiled. "Sure and be patient. We're so near success, and then a taste of ambrosia will have them all on their feet again."

Still the President hesitated, biting his lip. Mike Flynn spoke softly in his ear. "Power. Remember? Power is in making decisions and never wavering."

The fat man straightened his shoulders. "You are right. Sons, you will take her away and mount a guard below the Cascades. No arguing now. I have spoken."

There were three of them, all big men, and Moira let them lead her back up the stony valley to the waterfall. "Climb," they told her. One threatened her with a ham-like fist, and one with mean eyes and smile that were worse.

She climbed up into the chilly darkness beside the falls, feeling for hand and footholds, her mind numbed by the roaring force of the water beside her. By the time she reached the top her heart was pounding in spite of the oxygen pill. She was tired and cold and betrayed. Maybe it was only a game to him, but Mike had never done that to her before.

She lay on the ground at the top of the scarp and cried. She wept her frustration and loneliness to the empty Galaxy. Above her strange stars shone coldly and the aurora flickered green and red.

"Please don't cry like that."

A boy's voice, unexpectedly out of the darkness below her, startled her so much that she did stop. She raised her head, sniffed and stared.

A bulky shape, dark moving in the dark, heaved itself up from the depths beside the waterfall. He crawled over the rim and came to where she sat.

"My name is David N'Kumo, and I've come to help you."

Moira brushed a hand over her wet face. "N'Kumo? Really? David. Not Jody?"

"No, he's my uncle. He's the one who was banished before. He went north and discovered a place called Bamboo Valley."

"I've been there, I think. A great grove of bamboo and a single waterfall?"

"Then you must have met the Guardian and Olwen." The voice was eager. "Uncle used to speak of them often, but not now. Only a little while ago we all heard Guardian's voice coming out of a box. He told us to work on the mountain and to leave the Sacred Cave unguarded. What is he like?"

"All gold and very tall."

"His voice was in a box no bigger than the palm of my hand. How strange. I wish I could see him with my own eyes. That would be something."

"You can. He is here. And I know he did not speak through any old box, and he never removed the taboo that he put on the mountains and the cave. They were for your protection. You have been tricked by Mike Flynn."

"The stranger?" There was a silence. Then the boy spoke hesitatingly. "I think he is a liar. He is all tricks. If you ask him a question he doesn't answer. He just makes some more magic. I ate some of that ambrosia, and my mouth watered for more and my stomach ached for it. But Uncle Jody said that it was devil's food and the man was from the devil too for all he knew, but not from the Guardian."

63

"He was right. Mike Flynn is not from the Guardian, and I should know, for he's my own father, though I blush to say it. And I've got to stop him and get him away from this place before he hurts your people any more. Come on, let's go and talk to Guardian about it. He'll know what to do, I'll be bound."

David drew back, pulling his hand out of hers. "All the way to the north? It is a long journey, and we might die or get lost . . ."

Moira laughed. "We don't have to go that far. He'll be right here over the rise. Reading through every book we've got, I'll be bound. He's in my flyer."

"Here?" He peered through the darkness. "Will it be a proper thing for me to do, to meet the *Guardian*? What shall I say? Should I kneel?"

She grabbed back his hand. It felt cold and clammy. She laughed and gave it a comforting squeeze. "You'll like him. He's a bit out of date, but really very nice."

He let her lead him back over the top of the col to the place where the flyer was parked. To David it looked like a dark boulder parked among boulders. But when Moira knocked it rang hollow like metal and a sudden rectangle of yellow light appeared.

Bathed in this light, shining with incredible brilliance, stood an immensely tall golden figure, his head almost grazing the ceiling, his two eyes flashing crystals. David gulped down the fear rising like a hard fruit in his throat and walked, as boldly as he could, forward to his first meeting with the Guardian of Isis.

Chapter Six

They talked and planned for half the night, and Guardian became quite lively as he looked at David, discerning all kinds of likenesses to his Uncle Jody. Between them they told Moira much of the history of Isis, and how under the government of Mark London a whole mirage of superstition had grown up to distort the reality of Guardian, the gentle robot, and Olwen, who had been Keeper of the Light in the days before there was a colony.

David explained their beliefs. "Just as there is night and day and summer and winter, so there is life and death, good and evil. Guardian is all that is good. It is he who protects us and keeps Isis in the sky. The other, That Old Woman, is death, who comes to us when we least expect it and takes us to her terrible kingdom at World's End . . ."

"Only that is not true, as Jody found out," Guardian said.

David nodded shyly. He had lost some of his nervousness, but he felt rather as if he were in a dream, born out of the memory of his uncle's strange stories.

In turn David learned that Isis was not a flat piece of land with chaos and black night around its edges, but a huge ball of rock that rolled, in more or less of a circle, around Ra, which in its turn was huge and hot, and not a small flat shining disc as they had thought. It took some getting used to.

Moira explained to him that all the other stars were huge and hot, and that around many of them too, rolled balls of rock, some of which were inhabited by humans from Earth, just as Isis was. It was hard to believe at first, but he knew that what Moira told him was not a lie like the stories the stranger told. He listened enthralled while she described strange creatures that she and Mike had come across in a lifetime's travelling.

"How wonderful! This place must seem very plain and dull to you after all those adventures."

"Dull? Oh, David, I think it's the prettiest place in the Galaxy." Which could have just been politeness, but he didn't think so. He felt himself staring at her dark hair and wanting to reach out and touch it . . .

"David! I was saying that now we *must* get Guardian to help us make a plan."

"Yes, of course." He tried to pull himself together and concentrate.

Before dawn Moira lifted the flyer from its perch on the col and settled it gently on the flat top of Lighthouse Mesa. The noise of the propulsion unit would be masked by the thunder of the water falling into the pool below the Cascades, and if any of Roger London's sons should happen to look up at that moment, they would see nothing more than a streak in the sky like a falling star.

Guardian guided the flyer into a landing. His night vision was far better than that of the two humans on board. "There's a flyer up here already," he observed as they gently bumped to a halt.

Moira peered over his shoulder at the video screen. There it was, barely visible, in the lee of the great metal framework of the Light, the original communicator between the planet and passing ships. "So that's where the old devil hid it! While we're here I'll put another spanner in the works. I'll disable his engine so he'll not sneak off without my knowing it."

Guardian opened the door on to black night.

"Oh, I nearly forgot." Moira gave a couple of tablets to David. "That'll help you breathe until we reach the valley." She turned to Guardian. "Wish us luck."

"It is an irrelevent and meaningless phrase. Nevertheless: Good Luck. I will take the flyer back to the Cascades, and keep radio alert and act on your signal as we decided."

The door slid shut behind Moira and David and for a moment they stood close together in the darkness, under stars that burned with a fiercer clarity in the thin atmosphere. Moira used her flashlight to find the entry button to the second flyer. It took only a few seconds to stride across to the control panel and remove a component. Without it the flyer would be as airworthy as a sack of potatoes.

"Now for the climb," she whispered to David after she'd closed the door again. "I hope you've a good head for heights. It looks like a monstrous way down." She reached out in the silence for his hand. "What's wrong?"

"This place is taboo. I know that you've explained that it isn't a real thing, but still, it is what we are taught, and I am afraid."

"I understand." She put her arm comfortingly around him. "You know the rules were made to protect the first settlers from the lack of oxygen and the high ultra-violet radiation. The valleys were safe. The mountains and the mesa were not. And a simple rule grew into a sacred taboo. It's no more than that, David."

"I do know. It is what Uncle Jody always said, but . . ."

"I know. All your life you've been told it was wrong. Don't worry. See, you're getting warmer already. The pill I gave you will help you use oxygen more efficiently, and since it is night there is no need to be afraid of the ultra-violet . . ."

She had to stop talking then, because David suddenly tightened his arms around her and kissed her full on the mouth. He tasted of sun and sweat and sweet grass. His lips were gentle. Now it was Moira who shivered.

Behind them an oblong of light appeared in the darkness, shocking in its suddenness, throwing their single shadow across the top of the mesa. "Is everything all right? Can you find the way down?" Guardian's voice was anxious.

Moira laughed shakily. "Yes, everything's all right. We're just going, Guardian."

The way down was not hard to find with the flashlight. It had been lasered into smooth steps many years before. Girl-size steps, Moira thought. Olwen steps. Now a little overgrown with a wiry growth of moss-like stuff.

What would it have been like to be alone on a planet, she wondered. Would it have been any lonelier than *her* life, running from place to place with the police forever at their heels? But at least for her, there had always been Mike. For better or worse.

It was a wild climb. The wind began to rise and poured like water down the Cascades, bouncing off the vertical wall of the mesa in unexpected gusts. Had they been able to see the scree-strewn slope that lay below them, they would probably never have made it. But darkness hid the depths and the fear, and they climbed doggedly down.

They reached the valley at the south-eastern foot of the mesa, just out of sight of the waterfall pool. How surprised Roger London's sons would be, Moira thought, when they found out that she was back.

David took her hand and led her round the base of the mesa towards the south. Here two blacknesses opened up in the wall of the mesa, just a little darker than the night outside. "The big one on the left is the shelter cave," he whispered. "And this is the Sacred Cave."

Moira could feel his hand become clammy in hers. She wasn't crazy about going into dark caves in the middle of the night herself, though she'd had to sleep in some pretty strange ones before now, on primitive planets around the galaxy. Caves that were the nesting place of snakes, or the home of huge blue-eyed hairy spiders. One that had been piled with skulls. She hadn't minded that one too much, but the spiders . . .

She swallowed and tried to speak cheerfully. "Sure and there's nothing in there to be afraid of. It is only the old communications centre. Guardian was afraid that it might be damaged after he and Olwen left, and it was the only link between them and the settlers, so he forbade them to go in. That's all it is."

"Yes." David's breath was warm in her ear. "That's all it is. So why are you trembling?"

"I hate spiders."

He laughed. "Give me your light and I'll go first and make sure there are none."

It was a very nice cave, clean and dry without a single spider. The communicator filled the back wall, an old-fashioned model that made Moira stare. To the left of the entrance a beautifully carved table held a collection of rubbish. There was a burnt-out fluorescent tube, a replacement module for the communicator, a surveyor's stake, a work manual for the communicator. The only thing that wasn't rubbish was a laser, a heavy old-fashioned thing, but still usable.

After a quick look round Moira collapsed on to the rush mat that covered the cave floor. "Lord, but I'm tired! It's a while since I've been mountain climbing. And you—you've never climbed before, David—you were wonderful."

He shrugged off the compliment. "Tell me about this thing we must take from your father—what is it, this power?"

"It's a force field and matter transmitter. See, I have one too. They're mighty useful things on strange planets. They'll protect you from snake-bites and stray bullets, and cosmic radiation and the stones of angry farmers. Like an invisible shield."

"I think I can understand that. It's a kind of magic, isn't it? But what is a matter transmitter?"

"Oh, it's much too complicated for me to explain. All I know is that it works. If I'm a long way from the ship, for instance, and out of water, I can refill my waterbag from the ship's tank—a sort of remote control."

"You could get ambrosia into an empty box?"

"Exactly. Mike must have stolen a supply of honeycake before we left Quateb and hidden it on the ship. Then all he had to do was to transmit it down into an empty box, cake by cake. But it uses up a tremendous amount of energy, the matter transmitter."

"He says he's going to supply it to us for ever. How can he do that if he's only got a little?"

"It's just a promise with no truth in it, David."

"Why?"

"It's a trick, that's all. When you've mined out all the firestones you can find and you're busy building your Forever Machine, he'll take off. And your lovely machine won't work. So you take it apart to see what went wrong and you'll find the firestones aren't in it any more."

"But how could he take the firestones out without us seeing?"

"The matter transmitter again. Up into the hold of *The Luck of the Irish*."

David stared. This kind of wickedness was something new. Then he remembered that Mike had taught the children to trap larks just for the fun of it, and he believed Moira.

"It's not your fault he's like that."

"I know. But I still feel guilty. He's my responsibility."

"Ours," he said, and Moira felt warm inside. "So we have to steal his belt, is that it?"

"Yes, David. Without it he's nothing but a lot of words and a few cheap conjuring tricks he's picked up in bars around the galaxy."

"All right then." He kissed her forehead and they sat in comfortable silence for a little while.

Then Moira sighed. "It'll be daylight soon, won't it? We've got to think of a plan for getting the belt off him. He wears it awake and sleeping too."

David thought for a while. "Couldn't he be persuaded to go swimming in the pool? Then when he was in the water we could snatch it and . . . What's so funny?"

"Just you don't know my Dad," Moira gasped. "He hates water, inside and out. And cold water most of all. We'll have to get the clothes off him some other way."

"Hmm." David paused. Then he chuckled to himself. "What about fire ants?"

"They're not dangerous, are they?"

"Oh, no. But their bite is like fire and a person'll do anything to cool off. Even jump in the lake. But will the force field stop them biting? Bother." He put his hands to his head. "It goes round and round," he complained. "You can't get at him unless he's not wearing the belt, and you can't get the belt unless . . ."

"No. look. Suppose the fire ants were on the *inside* of his clothes, with the belt on top, it wouldn't stop them. That could work. Only how do we get fire ants *inside* his clothes?"

"If they were in his breeches . . . it'd take a little while for them to get warm. They only bite when they're warm."

Moira giggled. "Oh, I can see it now! But, David, can it be done? You'll never get inside the President's house unnoticed, will you? And who's to say the ants will stay put for the rest of the night."

"I thought I could be waiting in the washroom block early in the morning, before he wakes up. If I'm quick enough, and he's still sleepy, I don't think he'll even know it was me."

"Oh my stars! How long before they bite?"

"He'll have time enough to pull on his breeches and get out of there. Then he'll start to feel as if he were on fire. Whether he likes it or not, he'll tear off his clothes and jump in, I promise you."

"And one of us must be there to grab the belt and run. That'll have to be you too, David. I daren't be seen in the village."

71

"I want to do it. Anything to change the way we live now. Even the old hard ways and the taboos were better."

"We'll make Isis better, much better," Moira promised. "Can you swim?"

"Faster than anyone on Isis."

"Then you could dive into the lake and swim across to the western shore. I'll be waiting in the orchard, for you to throw me the belt. Then I'll run to the cave here, pick up my own belt and climb up the mesa to Dad's flyer. I'll take it across to the Cascades. Dad won't be long behind me, and I'll have the upper hand at last—both belts and both flyers."

"What do you mean—pick up your belt? Why don't you wear yours? You'll need protection too."

"I daren't wear it. Mike'll be expecting me to try something. He'll have tuned his belt to mine, and he'll know full well when I'm close by if I'm wearing it. It's not for long. Only from the orchard back to the Cave. After all, you have no protection at all."

"But it's my home and my life that I'm fighting him for."

"And it's my father who has spoiled everything here. Don't worry. I'll leave my belt and the module out of Dad's flyer here on the table. Among the other junk they'll never be noticed."

"Then I'd best go and collect some fire ants while it's still dark and they're asleep." He looked around the cave. "I'll take the cup, and then stuff the opening with grass. It'll keep them quiet until we're ready."

"Be careful, David. Mike's as sharp as nails and he's got eyes in the back of his head, as they say."

"*You* be careful." He slipped out of the passage and was gone like a dark shadow.

Moira was alone in the Sacred Cave, her mind whirling with thoughts, not all of which had to do with Mike and the job that lay ahead of them. She imagined what it would be like to live on Isis, to wake up every morning in the same bed, to be part of a community, to work, to have friends, to have someone to love . . .

Then she shook herself and told herself to stop mooning around and get on with it. She took the component from Mike's flyer and put it on the table and then, reluctantly, unfastened her jewelled belt and laid it beside the other things. She told herself she was silly to be afraid. This was a safe planet after all, with no weapons, no secret police, not even any dangerous animals. She didn't really need the belt; she just felt naked without it.

From the entrance of the cave she anxiously watched the eastern mountains. Slowly the sky above them lightened. Soon the sun would be up. Soon the village would waken. She left the cave and ran lightly through the grass towards the orchard that screened the western side of the lake.

A light appeared in the kitchens, another in the dining hall. Soon grey figures appeared from the houses, made for the wash house and then for the dining hall. Later she saw them again, stumbling up the stony slope towards the eastern flank where the vein of firestone was. They walked as if they were still asleep, but there was no overseer, no man with a whip. The only whip was their own senseless dream.

"Forever Machine," muttered Moira. "Damn you, Mike Flynn. No more. After today no more!"

The light strengthened until the lights in the windows faded. The sun burst above the mountains and sent long shadows rippling over the houses and down to the edge of the water. Moira had her eye fixed on the door of the President's house. "Come on, you lazy devil. Stir yourself."

She was hungry and thirsty and the water of the lake was tantalizingly close. But her silvery suit would be as visible as Saturn in Titan's sky against the shadows of the trees.

And there he was! Small, slim, a gaudy red-gold figure among the brown homespun of the other settlers, walking smartly from the London house to the washroom block.

Be ready, David, Moira prayed. She stood, pressed

against the rough bark of the tree. Her heart pounded her ribs. Her eyes watered with staring. Come on, slow coach!

There he was again, thumbs casually hooked through the jewelled belt, strolling back across the open green, like a lord of the earth. He was whistling. She could hear the shrill notes of 'A Wild Colonial Boy' clear across the lake. Everything was good in Mike Flynn's world. Disappointment tasted bitter in Moira's mouth. What had gone wrong?

Then she saw her father stop. He looked around. He shook his left leg. Then his right. More vigorously. He looked for all the world as if he were about to dance a jig. Moira felt a wild giggle rise in her throat and she stuffed her knuckles into her mouth.

It happened exactly as David had said it would. Mike looked wildly round, saw the silver gleam of the lake and raced towards it, scattering sleepy people on their way to breakfast. He moved in ungainly hopping strides, tearing off his clothes as he went. His doublet, his shoes, his breeches, his underclothes joined the trail.

Everyone stood openmouthed to watch the performance. Only Moira saw the dark figure of David streak from the wash house, scoop up the belt and head for the lake. His body, brown and muscular, hit the water at the same instant as Mike, pale and skinny, thrashed into it, fighting and splashing and swearing.

David was halfway across the lake before the heat of the ant bites cooled and Mike's wits came back. "Me belt!" he screamed. "Stop him! The boy's got me belt."

He floundered out of the water, pallid and enraged, causing scandalized screams and averted faces from the women in the crowd. He snatched at his breeches, held out to him helpfully by a small boy, grinning from ear to ear. "They were full of fire ants," the boy volunteered.

"Catch him!" Mike ordered, pivoting about on one leg, while he tried to push the other, wet and cold, into his breeches. "Swim after him, can't you?"

"David's the best swimmer in the valley. None of us'll catch him. Besides, look—she's got it."

Mike whirled around in time to see David throw the belt overarm, so that it flashed through the air in a rainbow curve of sun-caught jewels and water drops. Moira snatched the belt from the air and in the same movement turned and ran. Mike swore a string of colourful Irish oaths which no one in his audience understood.

"Me wand," he screamed. "Give me my wand."

Roger London stared palely at him.

"Me wand, you imbecile." Mike snatched it from him and pointed it like a gun at the small silver shape of Moira. She was out of the trees now and making good speed through the grass towards the mesa.

David reached the far side of the lake and pulled himself out onto the grass at the foot of the trees. He paused for an instant on one knee, bent over, gasping for air.

He heard a noise, as fast as a lightning stroke, harsh as falling rock. He felt the energy beam that burned as straight as an arrow from Mike's wand to connect the silver figure of Moira. For the space of two breaths he saw her run on. Then she fell face down in the long grass.

David ran, the stitch in his side forgotten, dodging through the trees, slipping on windfalls. He heard, a long way off, a repetition of the same dreadful sound. He felt, between his shoulder blades, a burning pain, like the bite of a fire ant. His arms and legs tingled and went numb. He stumbled, then recovered and ran on.

He was the fastest runner on Isis, but it seemed to take a lifetime to cover the distance between the orchard and the place where Moira lay in the autumn grass. He had time to feel a fierce anger against the man who would do this to his own daughter. He felt a freezing fear for the power he did not understand, that could reach right out from the white wand to drop her in her tracks. Beyond the anger and fear was a most terrible pain. If she should be dead, then he had found the one person he wished to share the rest of his life with, and in the same day lost her.

He was sobbing for breath by the time he reached the place where she lay cushioned in the deep grass. She was quite still, the dry grass splayed out from under her body. The only thing red that he could see were seed heads, crushed down by the force of her fall. There was no burn mark, no blood. Nothing to show where the Power had struck her.

He turned her over gently, half afraid of what he might see, and lifted the black hair away from her face. He touched her neck to feel the place where life throbbed. Suppose it was not there? His fingers trembled and he could feel nothing at all. But then it was there, slow and regular, the throb of life. It was just as if she were asleep. David burst into unaccustomed tears and held her body close in his arms.

The faint sound of shouting from across the lake brought him back to reality. He looked over his shoulder. People were running along the shore, making for the place where stepping stones forded the river. He looked down. The belt was clasped tightly in Moira's unconscious hand. Even in falling she had not let it go.

To take the Power from Mike Flynn. That was what was important. More important even than Moira. He pried open her fingers and caught up the belt. Then, doubled over so that he could not be seen above the high grass, he crept as fast as he could towards the foot of the mesa.

By the time he had reached the end of the long grass everyone had crossed the river. He still had to cover a short stretch of turf and scree where he would be visible to anyone happening to look that way. He prayed that they would not, and, thankful for his brown skin, lay flat and squirmed painfully over the last stony stretch.

By the time he reached the shadow of the Cave his mouth was full of dust and his knees were raw, but he was certain that he had not been seen.

Inside, he felt for the tinder-box, struck a spark, lit the tinder and blew it into flame. He lit the candle, carefully extinguished the tinder and returned it to its box. He must hide the belts, the one he had and Moira's. For he knew that Mike would never rest until he had his Power back, and he would have every person on Isis looking at each separate blade of grass in the valley until it was found. The sacredness of the Cave would not stop him from ransacking it.

He looked around desperately. Where? Where? His eye fell on the jug, three quarters full of stale water, faintly filmed with stone dust. He coiled the belts and dropped them into the water. Now the water gleamed where it had been opaque. He scraped at the floor with his fingers until he had a pinch of stone dust to drop on the surface. It spread and reflected the candle light with a dull bloom, as if it had been untouched for weeks. He pinched out the candle and blew on it to cool it. Let's hope no one will think of the Cave for a while, he thought, not until the candle is entirely cold.

Then he stood in the darkness of the entrance and watched the hunt below. The long grass shivered and bent. He could see heads and shoulders bobbing up and down as people thrashed through the thick grass. There was a shout and the heads and shoulders began to come together, like ants to a piece of honeycomb. Now was the moment, now, when no one would be looking this way.

He slipped through the opening and fled to the left, close to the mesa, where the cracks and folds of the ancient rock made vertical man-shadows. He moved fast but very quietly so that not a stone should slip to attract attention from what was happening down there among the grass.

Soon he was hidden from the eyes of the searchers, though not from the toilers on the mountain side. But they need not concern him. They would have eyes for nothing but the hammer, the red rock and the hope of the blue flash of firestone and the promise of a reward of ambrosia. If he

77

had not met Moira he might be up there now with the others. He cursed himself for his stupidity, for the stupidity of everyone on Isis.

The valley narrowed into shadow, cut by the silver knife of the Cascades. That was the way to go, to freedom and the Guardian. Guardian would know what to do.

But Roger's sons still guarded the way out of the valley. How was he to get past them? He bit his lip, trying to think of a plan.

There were three of them. John, the eldest, was a feeble copy of his feeble father, Chris was a big raw-boned fellow like his grandfather. And there was Charlie. Charlie was smaller, with a mean streak running through him, and he was disliked by almost everyone on Isis. The thought of Charlie touching Moira, dragging her against her will up the path from the village, made him angry all over again. It was seeing Charlie's hands on the strange girl, as much as his curiosity, that had made him follow her up out of the valley the night before.

John, Chris, Charlie. Against him . . . Then he nearly laughed out loud. Stupid! They're not guarding the way *out* of the valley, but the way back *in*. They didn't know, because nobody had had time in all the excitement to tell them, that Moira *was* back in the valley.

Quietly David back-tracked and slid down the screed slope until he was near river level. Then he ran forward, kicking stones, making as much noise as he could.

"Chris! Charlie! John!" He shouted above the noise of falling water, and at last attracted their attention. He staggered the last few paces and fell to his knees as if exhausted. "The girl . . . she's back in the valley . . . stole the stranger's belt. They've caught her again, but you're wanted."

"Who says?" That was Charlie, as belligerent as ever.

"Your father, of course. Who else?"

"Why'd he send you?"

"Because I'm the fastest runner, of course. You know that."
He put his hand to his side as if he had a stitch.

John and Chris looked at Charlie. Charlie nodded. "Right.
You'd better come with us, young David. Because if this is one
of your crazy stories I'm going to whip you raw. There's no
way the girl could have got past us."

"I don't know about that. But it's not a story, Charlie,
honestly. And I can't move until I've caught my breath and had
a drink. Where am I to go to anyway? Up there?" He jerked his
thumb at the Cascades and laughed.

"Just remember what I said, then. If you're lying I'll get you."

David remained sprawled on the rock until they were out of
sight. Then he slipped into the icy pool and swam across to the
eastern side. This seemed to be a day for getting wet. Not that it
mattered, except that climbing would be more difficult with
wet feet and hands.

He rubbed his hands as dry as he could on his hair, and then
began the dangerous climb, his ears straining to hear, beyond
the incessant roar of the falls, an angry yell that would warn
him that they'd come back, that he'd been seen.

But it didn't happen. His hands grasped the top. His legs
scrambled and swung and then he was over, rolling to the
safety of the stony col.

He caught his breath, staring up at the sky, and then rolled
over to look down into the valley, seeing it for the first time in
his life, from the heights. He could see the people flocking back
to the village. He could see the tiny figure they carried, too
small to be identified, but which must be Moira.

He could also see the three small dots that were the London
boys, hurrying to meet the others. Soon they would hear the
truth. They would know that it had been he who had stolen the
stranger's Power. Then they'd know they'd been tricked and
they'd be back, as Charlie had promised. He was safe up here,
but he didn't know how he was ever going to get back into the
valley to rescue Moira.

Chapter Seven

Moira was dreaming that she was sitting with her hands and feet in an Oldivian ant-hill. They were stinging her to death and it was all Mike's fault. She tried to get away, but she was tied down. She cried out. And woke up.

The pain was still going on, an agony of pins and needles in feet and hands. Mike was sitting beside her. He no longer looked like a puckish Irish boy, but a tired middle-aged man.

"Oh, me darling, is it hurting you bad?"

"You could have killed me, Dad," she gasped, and caught her lower lip between her teeth. The pain made her want to cry, and the despair of having failed was worse.

"That's a terrible fierce thing to say to your father. You know I'd never hurt a hair on your lovely head—on purpose, that is. It was seeing me belt torn from me body, so to speak, made me lose me head a trifle. But it couldn't have hurt you that bad, for there was little enough power left in the wand, not even enough to stop the boy."

Moira felt her face light up, and quickly turned her expression into a grimace of pain. So he hadn't been able to stop David! She swung her feet to the floor. "Help me walk off the cramps, Dad. The pain is killing me."

"You're fussing about nothing, aren't you?" He peered at her anxiously. "I'll swear it could be hurting no worse than whatever that boy planted in me breeches. Oh, that was a

80

wicked thing to do to your own Dad. Not just the pain, you understand, but to humiliate me so before all the people."

In spite of her pain Moira giggled. She hobbled up and down the tiny room until her legs began to feel as if they belonged to her again. "Oh, Mike, to see you hopping into that lake mother naked, it was the funniest sight of my whole life. And did you have a refreshing swim then?"

He flushed and pulled away the arm that supported her. "You'll come to a bad end, me girl, mocking your father like that."

"Worse than we've come to here?" Moira's face was suddenly grave again. "Spoiling the lives of innocent people? Turning them into slaves?"

"You're exaggerating, girl. Wait until they find me my belt again. I'll help them build their Forever Machine and we'll be out of here in a jiff."

"Oh, Dad! No machine. No more capers. Let's leave *now*. Let's tell the truth and get out of here. There are plenty of planets in the Galaxy where we can turn a penny without hurting honest folk."

"I'm sick of turning pennies, me girl. It's gold I'm after, and gold I will have.

"I won't let you do it."

"You can't stop me. Do you know where you are, Moira Flynn? Just look around you. You're in jail, me dear."

Moira had awakened thinking she was in one of the simple bamboo houses where most of the people on Isis lived. Now she saw that this was an unfinished, unfurnished house, and that the single window was barred with tough bamboo canes. She turned from the window in time to see Mike whisk through the door and slam it behind him.

"Mike, no." She ran to the door, lifted the latch and pulled. It was jerked out of her grasp and she heard the thunk of a bar falling into place. "Oh, Mike, please."

"I'll come for you the second I'm ready to leave. It'll not be more than a few days, so rest easy. There's a cot for your

81

comfort and washing things behind the screen."

"No!" She shook the door, but it didn't budge.

"You've slept in plenty worse places, me dear."

"Sure I have, Mike." She was in tears now. "But when the door was locked and barred you and I were on the same side of it."

He didn't answer.

"Mike!" She ran to the window and craned her neck as far as she could, standing on tiptoe, holding on to the bars. But Mike had gone.

"Mike, you let me out of here!" she yelled to the empty air, and then she sat down on the narrow cot and cried until her anger was gone. When she was finished she blew her nose and washed her face in the basin behind the screen. Then she walked up and down and tried to think.

Mike had not found his belt. *That* was the most important fact. When she'd fallen the belt had been in her hand. Oh, if only she'd thought to take a second and put it on, he'd have had no power over her. But she hadn't. She'd thought only of running.

If Mike didn't have the belt, then David must. And if he had it the game wasn't over yet, by no means. If only she could get out of here.

How stupid! She had only to call on Guardian and he'd rescue her. She put her hand on her left wrist and then looked down in dismay. Her communicator was gone. Oh, Mike, you devil, you've thought of every last thing, haven't you?

She strode to the window. It seemed that she was at the southern end of the village, for beyond the houses she could just see the rocky defile that led to the Cascades. She couldn't see the lake, which must be over to the left somewhere, but when she craned her neck she could just see, beyond the right hand frame of the window, the rock face where the people of Isis still toiled on for firestones.

Directly ahead of her was an aviary, an odd sight in a place like this. She could see the larks huddled on their perches. An occasional 'peep' came from them, as they ruffled up their back feathers and tucked their beaks beneath their wings. No glorious song, such as David had described to her. She could sympathize. She didn't feel like singing herself with the bars between her and the blue sky.

She shook the window frame, but the bars had been newly lashed to it with a rope too tough and wiry to pull apart. Oh, holy saints, if only I'd a knife on me, she thought. A knife and a strong arm to help. Jody N'Kumo . . .

Sooner or later someone was going to have to come by, and she would just have to hope that it would be someone she could trust, someone who would take a message to this man Jody, David's uncle.

In the meantime there was nothing for her to do but wait, and worry about David. Where was he? Surely, if he were free, he would have come for her already? But suppose he were in prison too? Oh, dear, how many prisons were there on Isis?

She stood at the barred window and stared until her eyes watered. Yet, in the end, she almost missed the one person who did come to the south end of the village in the whole of the long sultry afternoon, because the person was so small. She was just a dumpling of a girl with a full homespun skirt and apron, two tight braids and a little cap on top.

She scuttled between the houses like a small round shadow, ignoring Moira's prison, her mind obviously on something else. She made for the aviary, and Moira could hear her soft voice, but whether she was talking to herself or to the birds she couldn't tell. All she could hear was a mutter and a sniffle. The little girl shook the aviary door as if she were trying to open it. Then the mutters and the sniffles began again.

"Hey!" Moira called in a loud whisper that she hoped would go far enough, but not too far.

The little girl paid no attention; she was sobbing now.

83

"Help! Please!" Moira shouted.

The problem was that the wind was coming strongly out of the north, tossing her voice uselessly away. It was odd that the wind should be so strong and yet the air feel hot and heavy. But if the little girl couldn't hear her for the wind, then neither could anyone else.

"HEY!!!"

The girl started and looked guiltily around. Moira slipped her arm between the bars and waved frantically. Thank goodness! The little girl scrambled to her feet and came running, her dress blowing out like a parachute. She stopped beneath Moira's window. Her face was blotched with tears.

"Oh, dear, whatever is the matter!" Moira almost forgot her own predicament.

"Lars and Grant and the others caught the larks and put them in the cage. The stranger said they'd sing for us whenever we wanted, but it isn't true."

"Of course not. They won't sing when they're unhappy."

"I know. I tried to let them out but I can't. David said he'd help me, but that was days and days ago."

"I expect he forgot. Have you seen David?"

"No, but everyone's mad at him. Do you want me to find him?" She turned.

"No, don't go." Moira felt a sudden panic, as if this girl was the only human being in the world. "I don't think you *could* find David. But what about Jody N'Kumo? Could you ask him to come here?"

"Oh, no!" The eyes widened. "Nobody's allowed to talk to *him*."

"Why?"

"Because Jody tried to stop the stranger and said he was telling lies and that the Guardian hadn't talked . . ." She stopped suddenly and began to suck her thumb, while her other hand twisted the corner of her apron.

"Hey, don't be afraid. What's your name?"

"Marianne Oluk." She bobbed a curtsey.

84

"And I'm Moira Flynn. You're a big girl, Marianne, aren't you? How old are you?"

"I'll be four at Thanksgiving time."

"Really?" Then Moira remembered that Isis had a much longer year than Earth, so that the little girl was probably about six. Old enough to be an ally?

"So what did the President do to Uncle Jody?" she asked, hoping the little girl wouldn't be scared again.

"Shut him up in his house."

"Poor Uncle Jody. I wish I could help him, and the larks too, but I'm shut in here myself."

"Why don't you go out the door?"

"It won't open. Maybe it's stuck. Would you go around and see if you can unfasten it for me?"

"All right." She skipped out of sight. Moira had to bite her lip to stop herself from crying out to Marianne to come back where she could see her.

It seemed ages, though it couldn't have been more than a minute or two, before she skipped back into sight.

"Well?"

"There's a big stick right across the door and I can't reach it."

Moira thought for a while. "Marianne, could you do something for me? Something grown up and real. Maybe difficult and a bit scary."

"Oh. I don't know." The thumb went back in the mouth.

"I'm in prison, like the larks. Won't you help me get out, and then I'll let the birds go?"

Marianne smiled. "I'd like that. Will you really free the birds?"

"I promise."

"All right. What do you want me to do?"

"Can you sneak into the kitchens without anyone noticing and borrow a knife? Then bring it to me without anyone knowing. Could you do that?"

"I think so."

"You'll have to be really careful that no one sees you. And, Marianne . . . " The little girl had turned and begun to run. "Marianne, a *sharp* knife," she yelled.

Marianne vanished between the houses without looking back. Could she do it? Suppose her return were to coincide with a jailer bringing a meal—supposing Mike were not to starve her. What was the time anyway? It must be afternoon, since all the shadows fell to the right. But how late? Dinner time?

Moira walked across the room. Five paces to the wall. And back. Five paces to the window. Nothing to see but the miners slaving away at the red rock on the mountain. Five strides to the wall. Five to the window. What time was it? The shadows were not that long, but there was a red glow in the air.

Surely Marianne would have the sense to hide if she were to see one of the grown-ups with a food tray. Why was it taking her so long? Taking a knife shouldn't be that difficult. Children could usually sneak in and out of places without being noticed.

Five paces away from the window. Five paces back. Her hands clenched the bars. Oh, come on!

It was definitely getting darker . . .

There she was! Scuttling between the houses all out of breath, with her dress blowing in front of her and the hair teased out of her tight braids so it blew in a tangle around her pink face.

"I'm sorry I was so long. All the grown-ups are standing around shouting at each other. I've never seen anything like it." She put a hand to her side. "Oh, but I've got a stitch. It seems no one can find the stranger's Power, though they've searched the whole valley. And David's gone too. The stranger swears that it is David who stole his Power. And some of Jody N'Kumo's friends are saying maybe he was right all along, and that the stranger's a liar and he's not from the Guardian but from some other place. Only the rest are

86

paying no attention, and Jody is still locked up."

"You're a brave girl. Have you got the knife safely?" She stood on tiptoe to wriggle her arm down through the bars. "Reach up and put it in my hand."

"I can't reach that far."

"Hold the knife upright by its handle, but steady, please. I'll try and reach the blade."

The trouble was that she couldn't see. In the end she just let her hand dangle loosely from the window until she felt the cold metal touch her palm. She curled her fingers carefully around it. "All right, Marianne. I think I've got it."

"Ah-hooo . . . Ah-hooo . . . Ah-hooo . . ." The long-drawn-out note of a horn came riding on the back of the wind and was torn to shreds among the houses.

Marianne screamed and turned. Moira's hand tightened on the blade at the same instant and she felt the sting of steel across her palm. Automatically her hand flew open. The knife fell.

"Marianne!"

The little girl had gathered up her skirt in both hands. She cried over her shoulder. "The three-note has sounded. I must get to the Shelter Cave quickly or That Old Woman will get me."

"The knife first. Marianne, *please* . . ." But she was talking to the wind. Marianne had gone.

Now Moira could see a turmoil of people, all running north and west, towards the river. Narrowing her eyes against the wind she looked east. The ant-like miners had suddenly become individuals again. They were throwing down their tools, running along the platforms, scrambling down the ladders, pouring in hundreds down the slope past the cemetery.

The three-note. The Shelter Cave. If only she could make sense of Marianne's words. In spite of Guardian's and David's coaching she didn't know enough about this planet, that was the trouble. That Old Woman—wasn't that how they talked of death? Maybe the three-note was more than just the signal for some sort of ceremony. Maybe it was a warning. Like earthquake, or flood or fire . . .

The eastern slope was deserted now. There was nobody left but herself. Forgotten? Or deliberately left to face whatever was coming. That Old Woman . . .

Oh, come on, Moira, she scolded herself. But the fingers that clung to the bars were suddenly slippery with sweat. She drew her hands in to wipe them. It wasn't sweat after all, but blood from the knife cut across her palm.

She washed the wound and bound it with a strip torn from the hand towel left by the basin. Then she went back to the window. When she stood on tiptoe, her chin wedged on the sill and her face pushed right up against the bars, she could see the ground almost up to the wall below the window.

But she couldn't see the knife. It must be lying very close to the wall, maybe only a few centimetres away. Only the wall between. She fell to her knees on the dirt floor, her hand against the bamboo wall. So close. Almost close enough to touch . . .

The wind was howling like a banshee now, like the ghosts of all the avenging souls whom Mike had robbed or crossed or conned. It screamed through the cracks and along the floor.

Along the floor! So there was no foundation. Her fingers felt below the lowest pole. Why, if she could only dig a hole beneath the wall she would be able to reach through to the knife on the other side. If she only had a knife to dig with!

She began to claw at the earth with her fingernails, but the dirt floor had been too firmly packed. The house shook in sudden gusts of wind that were like a giant's breath. At this rate it would fall to pieces around her and she'd no longer have to worry about being in prison. But she could be dead.

The wind reached a screaming crescendo and she jumped to her feet in time to see a column of red dust, whirling like a drunken devil, waver down the valley towards her. It veered suddenly to the right and licked hungrily along the rock surface where the miners had been working.

As it passed the platforms seemed to explode. The ladders were sucked up, shaken and dropped to the ground in a hail of bamboo shreds. Then the dust devil was gone and with it every trace that men had ever touched the eastern slope, except that where the hammers had broken the rock the colour was a brighter red, as though the mountain was bleeding.

Moira shivered. It was clear that the storm was coming directly out of the north, funnelled down the col above the Cascades, squeezed between the eastern wall and the mesa, and forced down the river valley, to explode like a shotgun blast upon the village.

And she was in the direct line of the storm. It was only luck—the luck of the Irish, Mike would say—that had diverted the first dust devil to the east, away from her prison.

A knife. What could she use to dig with instead of a knife? There was nothing except the cot and the toilet things behind the screen. Yes! She threw the screen aside, grabbed the pitcher and hit it against the basin as hard as she could. It broke satisfyingly into half a dozen pieces. She chose the one with the sharpest point and ran back to the window.

The shard would never have been sharp enough to cut the tough fibres that lashed the bars to the window frame, but it made a terrific trowel, and she gouged and scooped at the hard dirt of the floor.

Once she was through the top layer of packed dirt the going was easier. It wasn't long before she had a curved tunnel leading under the wall. She lay on her front and slipped her unbandaged hand through the opening. She could feel wiry grass prickle at her wrist. But nothing else.

Doggedly she scooped and dug, making the tunnel wider and longer, so that she could get her whole arm through. The house shook and the terrible many-voiced scream of a dust-devil was upon her. She dug frantically, flinging the dirt to right and left. She could see light now, and the wind came in like a torrent. Now she could get her arm right through.

There was a tearing sound close by and a shuddering crash as something smashed into the wall just above her. But in that same instant her fingers closed around the handle of the knife. She wriggled carefully back with her prize.

It was a beauty. A paring knife, very old, its blade worn to a thin crescent from years of sharpening. She began to saw at the knots and wrappings of the bars. She cut the last strand and pushed triumphantly. Nothing happened and for a minute she felt black despair.

Then she looked out and saw that the aviary had been blown by the wind to jam against the lower part of the frame. All it would take would be one good push. She looked around and grabbed the screen, folded it to its narrowest and, holding it like a battering ram, charged at the window.

One, two, three, wham! The shock ran up her arms into her shoulders. But when she pulled back the screen the window bars fell. She was free!

She pushed the cot under the window, climbed on it and dived out, head first, her eyes screwed up against the wind and dust. Then she crawled across to the wreckage of the aviary.

She spent a few precious minutes sawing through the ropes that bound the aviary together, so that the birds could escape easily. Whether they would survive the wind she did not know. Two small bundles on the floor told her that not all of them had lived through being slammed up against the wall of the house. There was nothing more she could do for the others but trust that their instincts would keep them safe. Anyway, she'd kept her word to Marianne.

She stood up and the force of the storm hit her like a giant's hand and knocked her to her knees. She caught hold of the wall and clawed her way around to the south side, where there was an illusion of shelter, and time to think.

To think calmly. She took a shaky breath. She'd been in enough tough corners in her life to know a beauty when she saw it. It would take all her wits to survive this one. Where would she be safe?

The Shelter Cave was too far to the north and the way to it was too exposed. The older houses, the plastic foam ones, might do at a pinch, but even to reach them she would have to struggle through the teeth of the storm.

Or she might go south, like a ship running before the wind, and that was what her instincts told her to do. But what lay south? She peered between the shifting veils of red dust and saw reeds and marsh grass. A faint white gleam of something manmade. What was it?

Then she remembered what the Guardian had told her. The wall, through which the river ran. And sink holes, some small, some big enough to lose a child down . . . She began to run, the wind pushing at her back, stinging her with whips of red dust.

She stumbled over unseen tufts of wiry grass and felt water seep coldly into her shoes. But she was light and she never stayed long enough on one footfall to sink.

And there at last was the wall, smooth plastifoam, impossible to climb. But somewhere the river entered and she could go that way too. She felt her way towards where the ground was wettest.

There! She almost fell headlong. The sudden cold seeping through her jumpsuit made her gasp, but she flung herself down into it, and half-swimming, half-crawling, followed the river current.

The arch grazed her head and she ducked. It was suddenly so quiet beneath the water that she wished she could lie there for ever. But her lungs were bursting, and she raised her head again into the scream of the wind.

She crawled forward over the pockmarked gravel, feeling

cautiously with her hands. The river tugged eagerly at her body, and suddenly it fell away beneath her and she was hanging over a wide sink hole down which the water of the river poured.

She rolled to one side, out of danger, and lay on the stony ground, her heart pounding furiously. But only for a minute. The voice of the wind urged her on. She crawled forward again, exploring with her hands for a vent that would be big enough to shelter her without swallowing her up. There. That would do. Big enough for head and shoulders.

As her body blocked the entry hole, the storm was cut off as abruptly as if she'd turned a switch. The only sound, once her ears had recovered from the shock, was her own breathing, which echoed large and unearthly, like the breathing of an enormous underground monster.

It was dark, so dark that she might be blind. She waved her arms in front of her. She could feel them moving but she could see absolutely nothing. At the very extent of her fingertips there was cold damp rock and then space that went down and down for ever.

Chapter Eight

David lay on his stomach on the dry grass at the top of the Cascades. He had watched Moira being carried into a small new house at the south end of the village. He knew it well, for he had helped to build it for his sister Ruth and her husband-to-be. He longed to leap down the Cascades, run through the village, tear down the door and rescue his Moira. Only he couldn't. And she wasn't really his. He buried his face in the sweet dry grass.

A hard touch on his shoulder startled him and he rolled over and on to his knees. It was Guardian, brilliant in the early morning light.

"Did you succeed? Have you Michael Flynn's power belt?"

"Yes. But they got Moira." He explained quickly, while the smooth head nodded understandingly. ". . . and so I hid both belts in the Sacred Cave," he finished. "It seemed the best idea at the time."

"You have done very well. They will not harm Moira. Nothing in the history of your people indicates violence. Do you disagree?"

"Things have changed. I don't know if it's the stranger himself, or the taste of ambrosia. Maybe both." David hesitated. It was hard to put into words. "People quarrel like never before. The children are always squabbling over trifles. There's . . . there's greed in the valley."

93

"And you are afraid for Moira?"

"Yes."

"Do not be. I promise you that I will not allow violence, even if I have to break Olwen's edict to stop it. But we must wait for dark. You will eat and rest. Come. Once it is dark we will take Moira's flyer down to the marshes below the village and rescue her from her prison, if indeed she is in prison."

"Wait till *dark*? But . . ."

"Be patient. Come and sit in the shade of the flyer and I will make you a meal. Moira has the most agreeable-looking foodstuffs and a portable stove on which to prepare them."

He stalked off and David followed reluctantly.

Looking back, David would remember that day as the longest in his whole life. Guardian did his best. He fed David unusual little meals from the store in Moira's flyer. David would probably not even have touched the food, except that he thought—this is what *she* eats.

Guardian tried to teach him games, not only from Earth, but from other mathematically inclined planets; but his computer brain against David's lack of attention made for poor matches. He told him stories about the early days on Isis, about Olwen's parents and the little girl, and how he himself had been changed from being a run-of-the-mill Data Collecting and Processing Robot to being a Person, charged with the loving care of the infant Olwen. About half of David's mind found the stories fascinating. The other half obstinately and unceasingly worried about Moira.

By mid afternoon his body seemed to have caught the restlessness of his mind. He prowled up and down the stony col until he was out of breath. He played stone-hops on the river, but it flowed too fast for the game. At last the altitude made him cough and Guardian said his lips were turning blue and he must rest in the shadow of the flyer and breathe from its oxygen machine for a while.

"You're as bad as Olwen," Guardian scolded just like one

of the aunties, and David found it funny to hear the motherly words coming from the two-metre-high figure all shining gold. "I remember once, when things had gone wrong and she was unhappy, she walked up and down the terrace until I thought she would wear out her shoes. Though that time, I remember, it was not the worrying that made her restless but the approach of a storm, only we did not realise that at the time . . ."

He stopped talking so suddenly that David stared, wondering what had gone wrong. The golden robot stood like the golden statue of a god, and his crystal eyes did not shine outward any more, but were as dull as pebbles. David shivered.

"A *storm*! How foolish of me not to suspect," Guardian said in a perfectly normal tone of voice. He strode to the side of the col and began to climb the flank of the mountain to the left. David shaded his eyes against Ra's light and watched him.

Guardian had stopped and was staring intently towards the north. David stood up and stared too, but there seemed to be nothing to see but a tumble of red peaks and purple shadows and the silver thread of the river.

Then Guardian was standing beside him again. He had descended so quickly that David hadn't even noticed him, and the feel of his metal hand on David's arm made him start.

"A storm is coming. Why has the alarm not been sounded from the Cave?"

David stared, his mind confused.

"The light above the communicator warns you of approaching storms, does it not? That has not changed?" David nodded. "And there is always a person on watch to give the alarm so that you can take shelter?"

Now at last the meaning of what Guardian was saying got through the fog of misery and worry about Moira. "No. Michael Flynn got the President to remove the guard from

95

the Cave. He said it was a waste of time and that he needed every able-bodied man to hunt for firestones. He said the taboos could be ignored. He said *you* said so."

"You know that's not true."

"Yes. But . . ." David tried to avoid the crystal eyes that stared down at him.

"What is it? Why have you stopped trusting me? Are we not friends? I even shared my life with Olwen with you."

"I'm sorry. I didn't mean to hurt your feelings."

"That is irrelevant. What is the problem?"

"Wasn't it you who protected us from storms, and made the red light appear in the Sacred Cave? Yet for the last two years and more you were by Olwen's grave and the warnings have still come. How can the warning be in the Cave when you are here with me and you were surprised that the storm is coming?"

"You have more important things to worry about than that! After Olwen's death I coupled the weather sensors from the Light to the signal in the Cave. It is automatic. After her death there was no need for my intervention. It was she who was sensitive to storms and so could give the warning before the instruments could. Are you satisfied?"

"Yes. What are we to do? If no one is there to sound the three-note they'll be caught outside. There'll be no time to reach the cave." The reality sank slowly into David's mind. "I've got to go down and warn them." He ran to the south side of the col and swung his legs over the cliff above the Cascades.

"Wait." Guardian caught his arm. "We will save valuable time if I take Moira's flyer. I will drop you at the west side of the mesa, where no one will see us. You can run for the Cave and I will stay in the lee of the mountains where Moira's flyer will be protected from the storm."

"Suppose someone sees you?"

"Once the three-note has sounded no one will have eyes for anything but the Cave and the northern sky. Now hurry!"

David scrambled aboard and Guardian swung the flyer north around the mountains so as to approach the valley from the west, out of the afternoon sun. They dropped quickly down to the grassland and Guardian skimmed the surface until he found a place close beneath the south-western wall of the mesa.

Guardian was restless. "The valley is not a good place either. I would prefer to fly above the storm, but I do not yet understand how the fuel supply works. It would be a terrible thing to run short before she could return to her ship."

He was speaking to himself and David left him fussing and slid down to the ground. With a goodbye wave he set off at a steady jog along the scree-strewn slope at the bottom of the mesa. It did not take him long to reach the Cave and plunge down the dark passage. Sure enough the signal was on, a huge red eye that winked on and off, on and off, from the black shape of the cabinet that filled the back of the Cave.

David ran outside, blinking in the sudden light, and grasped the horn that hung directly outside the door. He took a deep breath.

Ah-hooo . . . Ah-hooo . . . Ah-hooo . . .

The sound returned to him from the eastern mountains, and the wall of the mesa hurled back the echo as if a dozen horns had been blown.

He squinted his eyes against the dazzle of light on the crimson cliffs to his left. Good, the workers had heard. Like ants shaken off a honey stick they were tumbling down the ladders, separate black dots running together into clots, the clots pressing together to form in the end a solid dark line of people all heading north to the stepping stones across the river. It was all right. The people would be safe.

He ducked back into the shadow of the passage, remembering that several people in the approaching crowd were after his blood—the stranger, Mike Flynn, and the three sons of the President, Chris and John and Charlie. He would hide until nearly everyone was in and then casually add himself on to a group, to look as if he had been working all day on the cliff face with them. Certainly he was tired and dusty enough to look the part.

Once inside the Cave he would see if he could get close to Moira. Then, as soon as the worst of the storm was over, he would get hold of her and together they would make a run for it, out of the cave and round the mesa to Guardian and the flyer. Moira would be safe.

It was a good scheme and he was proud of it. He felt almost happy, standing in the shadows watching the people come closer. Then, quite suddenly, while he waited, the last words of Guardian came back to him. 'It would be a terrible thing to run out of fuel before she can return to her ship.'

Return to her ship. How stupid he was. He was spending all his energy and risking his future on Isis to help Moira get rid of Mike Flynn. And all the time he was forgetting that the enemy was Moira's father. That where he went, she would go too. All because of a stupid promise. And he would never see her again in his whole life.

It was a loss such as he had never dreamed of. After all, on Isis you grew up in the valley, you fell in love, you married, you lived in the valley through good harvests and bad, until that final separation at the hands of That Old Woman.

But you'd always be together; there was no other way to be. Until now. Now in his mind he could see the starry sky going on for ever and ever, and in it somewhere, like a wandering star, the ship with Moira in it. One day very soon she was going to climb into the flyer and circle out of sight like the upland lark. One night soon he would look up at the six stars that made the Table. Then he would see the extra point of light, that was *her* ship, wink out of sight, out of space, out of time. For ever. He bit the knuckles of his hand.

There were voices close by. People pushed past the door, unaware that he was standing just an arm's stretch away.

The Council was in front, the President and Michael Flynn jostling to be in the first place. Good. That would mean that they would find places to sit at the very back of the cave, and be unlikely to notice him if he stayed close to the door.

He waited until almost everyone had gone by and then casually joined some men who were among the last to enter. They hurried, looking anxiously up at the sky above the mesa. Nobody paid any attention to him.

In the packed cave bunnyfat lamps burned on the high rock niches, giving a wavering light that was tossed to and fro as the winds eddied in through the opening. David edged away from the group he had come in with, and stood in a patch of shadow where he could see the faces of the remaining people as they entered.

Where was Moira? He was confident that he hadn't missed her. People ran in, in ones and twos now, breathless and windblown. Uncle Jody was bundled in, and pushed unceremoniously to the back. Where was Moira? The latecomers arrived coughing and spitting dust, eyes streaming. The storm was mounting.

In the old days the door would now be slid across the entrance to keep out wind and dust. But something had jammed the unknown mechanism and nothing had been done about it. Those standing close to the entrance had to endure the eddies of dust that swirled in as the wind howled down the valley from the north.

Where was she? Was it possible that she was still locked up and they had forgotten her? He wriggled boldly through the crowd, no longer caring who saw him. He pushed his way through to the very back, where there were benches against the walls. People were beginning to settle down for the long wait, each finding a small piece of floor to sit on, shaking sand from headscarves and beards, calming the children.

David picked his way among them, to lean over and catch the stranger by his fur-cloaked shoulder.

99

Mike Flynn turned. "What the . . .? Why, it's you—the boy who stole me Power!"

"Keep your voice down or you'll be sorry," David hissed. "Where's Moira?"

Mike Flynn was scowling, his mouth open to answer. He closed it. Swallowed. Looked round. "She . . . she must be here," he stammered.

"I cannot see her."

Mike Flynn's face seemed to shrink onto its bones. He stood up, his affectations dropping from him with his cloak. "Where's me daughter?" he thundered above the babble.

There was silence for an instant. Then a rustling, a muttering, as each person turned to look at those around him. Daughter? Since when did the stranger, holder of Power, have a daughter? Few of them had even seen Moira, except as a limp body.

"If you mean the girl," Chris London spoke up. "We put her in the new house at the bottom of the village."

"As you ordered us to, father," John whined.

"Give me patience!" Mike Flynn screamed. "I know that. Did I not talk to her myself? But did not one of you feather-brained dung-shovellers remember to let her out?"

"Did you remember?" David asked softly.

There was an awful silence.

Mike drew out a handkerchief and mopped his pale face. "How bad are these storms? She'll be safe down there, won't she?" The downcast eyes, the averted faces told him the truth. "Oh, holy angels, me daughter!" Then, at the top of his voice. "I'll pay any man a gold piece who'll bring her safe back to me."

At first there was silence. Then from the back of the crowd a voice muttered. "What about your power? If you're the Guardian's friend how come you didn't know about the storm?"

"I'd go for my own kin, not for gold," another voice put in, and there was an approving mutter.

100

David fought his way back through the crowd to the door. Across the heads Mike became aware of what he was doing. "Oh, good boy then. Forgive me for my cross words. It was just the heat of the moment. Bring her back to me."

David stared darkly back. "I'll find Moira for my sake and hers. And to keep her here with me, if I can. Not for you."

"She'll not stay. She'll follow her father as she's always done."

"You're no father. You're not fit." David shouted his anger and fear over the howling of the wind.

"She'll come when I call her. She'll follow me across the Galaxy. She promised . . ." Mike was pushing his way through the crowd after David. But now David had gone. Mike yelled after him, but the wind threw the words back in his face.

"She promised . . ." he muttered to himself, and tried to go back to his special place at the back, only now the people did not make room for him, and in the end he had to make do with a corner against the cave wall, to stand and wait, a small man in tawdry red and gold.

Once outside, it seemed to David that the wind was his ally. It pushed him between the shoulder blades, propelling him across the grassland and over the ruin of the cultivated fields almost as if he were flying. He hardly heard the scream of it as he ran on its wings.

By the time he reached the old bridge, built in the Before Times across the marshy river downstream from the village, he was out of breath. And now he and the wind were enemies. He turned north and fought it through the swamp and up the slope towards the outskirts of the village. The last house, the one ready for Ruth, once harvest was in . . .

But where was the house? Could he have lost his sense of direction in a village as familiar as the lines on his hand? At last, with a sense of horror, he began to understand that the splintered pile of bamboo ahead had been Ruth's house.

101

He crouched with his back to the wind, pulling poles from the debris and throwing them aside to be whirled away by the giant hand of the storm. He couldn't see properly, that was the trouble. The air was a redness full of sand that blinded the eyes. He felt rather than looked through the ruins, dreading what he might find.

There was nothing. Only a splintered bed frame, a broken pitcher and basin and the small bodies of a couple of birds lodged in the ruins. But she wasn't there. She had escaped. Only where had she gone?

David reached out with his mind and made the same connections that Moira had made earlier. There was only one possible safe place that she would have known of. She would have tried to reach it and he must follow her and make sure.

The last taboo. The thought flashed through David's mind as he slid into the river at the place where it vanished beneath the Wall. I have broken every other taboo on Isis, so why should I be afraid of this one? But a part of his mind dreaded the fearful secret that the Wall must enclose. The rest of him didn't care if it was monsters or the chaos of World's End, just so long as *she* was safe.

He swam downstream, the water washing the burning sand from his body, stinging on the raw patches. Its sound was friendly after the scream of the wind. He let it carry him along, and only just in time did he become aware of the danger. Only at the last instant did he roll to one side against the bank, clawing at the marsh grass, pulling himself to safety.

So this was the mystery! The river that nourished the valley was swallowed up by the open mouth of Isis itself. Isis drank its own river. And nearly made a meal of him too!

He crouched with his back against the wind and peered through the red gloom. He saw her almost at once. The whole enclosed area was dark, the colours weirdly altered by the ruddy sky. But her jump suit was still silver white, her legs a double line of white against the darkness, her body a shimmery patch, overlaid only at the creases with a drift of sand.

He crawled across the pocked ground to where she lay. For an agonizing instant it seemed to him that she was headless. His stomach turned over and something squeezed all the breath out of him so that he went black behind his eyes. Then he blinked and breathed deeply and made himself look again. And he saw that her head and shoulders were hidden in a hole like the one down which the river vanished, but smaller and dry.

He lay beside her, his arm over her hips. She shivered, and his heart leapt because she was still alive. He crept as close to her as he could, and buried his head in the gap between the drifting sand and the curve of her waist.

Above their two bodies the storm raged. Up on the mesa the old Light shook and the wires shrilled with a piercing note so high that it was almost inaudible.

Mike Flynn's flyer shivered. The wind nudged it south and it trembled as if it were alive. Slowly it moved closer to the edge. It teetered on the brink. Then the wind lifted it triumphantly and for an instant it seemed to be flying. But the wind drew back and took breath for another onslaught. In the space of that indrawn breath the flyer faltered, slipped sideways and spun down to crash into a thousand silver pieces among the rocks at the foot of the mesa.

The crash was borne on the wind and echoed round the valley. It almost seemed that that was what the storm had all been about, that now it had done its work it could stop. The gale died down to a brisk wind, with only an occasional buffet to remind one of its possibilities. From the racing clouds the red dust fell, coating everything with the stuff of Isis.

David lifted his head to look around and sneezed loudly. He pulled gently at Moira's waist, lifting her backwards to release her from the vent. She turned as soon as she was free and put her head against his chest.

"Oh, David, I knew you would come."

Chapter Nine

In the crowded Shelter Cave Mike Flynn stood alone. His red and gold clothing was coated with dust and his face was grey with fear where it was not grimed with red dust. His strange pale eyes searched the red inferno raging outside for any sign of life. From time to time his lips moved and he muttered, "Me darling. All me gold. Everything. The firestones, every last one of them, I swear. If you'll only bring her back."

His Power was gone. Everyone on Isis could see that, just by looking at him. To none was this sight more bitter than to Roger London. It had been within his grasp, this magic that he'd always lacked; and now this stupid man, sniffling for his daughter, had snatched it from him. Now there seemed to be no hope at all of regaining the Power that had been so sweet.

Roger London ground his teeth and listened sourly to the talk of that impossible man Jody N'Kumo. He and his upstart friends were saying that if they were to clean the sand from the grooves around the entrance and grease the strange machinery with bunnyfat, they would not have to endure the buffets of wind and the dust that continually blew in through the cave opening.

People were beginning to listen and agree, especially those who were closest to the door and suffered most from the dust. That upstart Jody! Ever since he had survived banishment and come back unscathed out of the hands of That Old Woman he thought he knew more about how to run Isis than his elders and betters.

The storm screamed to a crescendo, and then the beings from World's End hurled a thunderbolt directly at the people sheltering in the Cave. Everyone cowered back at the mighty crash and many screamed. But only Mike Flynn saw the silver shards of metal spin down in the red dust and only he knew what it really was. The knowledge undid him completely.

"Me flyer! Oh, holy saints, me flyer! In smithereens. And me daughter gone. And *her* flyer dear knows where. What am I to do?" And in front of them all the tricksy man, the man of Power, the friend of the Guardian of Isis, sank to his knees by the cave entrance, hid his face in his hands and began to weep.

Both Roger London and Jody N'Kumo knew the danger that Mike Flynn put himself in at that moment. No longer did he have the shield and protection of being a man apart. Now he was only a man . . . weeping. Roger London's pursy little mouth twisted into a smile, but he said nothing and made no move towards his enemy. Let him go on. Soon I'll be revenged. And maybe even gain back the Power.

Jody pushed through the crowd and into the emptiness around the stranger. He shook his shoulder. "Pull yourself together, man!" His voice was strong and deep, a voice of authority.

Mike's lament turned into words, "Me flyer gone, smashed to tiny pieces. Moira gone the Lord knows where . . . and how'm I to get back to my ship, tell me that? Oh, God help me, I'll be stuck on this awful planet for the rest of me natural days and *The Luck of the Irish* orbiting up there as sweet as you please and no way short of sprouting wings for me to get back to her." He raised his hands, shook his fists at the sky and tore at his pale hair.

"Stop it," Jody warned him, softly, but Mike ranted on.

105

"Marooned for me life at the back end of the Galaxy with an ignorant bunch of dung-shovelling farmers," he screamed against the wind, which chose that very instant to die away entirely, so that his howling words echoed clearly around the cave, to be heard by every person there.

Anger shivered through the crowd.

Now, thought Roger London, and stood up. It was his last chance to grasp the Power. He brought his right arm up slowly, in a gesture he vaguely remembered his father using with great effect, and pointed at Mike Flynn. "He is not from the Guardian. He has deceived us. Only hear how he speaks of our beloved Isis. He is evil. He belongs with That Old Woman and he should go back to her!"

Even his sons were surprised at the strength with which he shouted. Charlie and John and Chris had seen with anger and frustration the Power slip from their father's weak hands, and now they were quick to grab the opportunity to help him regain it. They'd work side by side to see him back where he belonged. Later, when things had settled down, they would fight over which one of the three would make the best President. For now they spoke with one voice.

"We must destroy evil."

"Root it out of the valley. Banish him."

"No. Banishment is not enough." Charlie spoke quietly into a sudden attentive silence. "We must get rid of him for ever."

By the door Jody shook the kneeling man. "Get up. Go on. While you've still got time. Run for it!"

But Mike Flynn, shrivelled, small and as dusty as a storm-tossed bird, only cowered against Jody and clung to his legs. "They're mad. They'll kill me. You've got stop them. Please save me. I'll give you gold, firestones . . ."

"Stupid. As if I cared . . ." Jody broke off with an impatient exclamation. "Run now, while you still have a chance. Make for the Cascades." He kept his voice low. "I'll try and hold them back."

A voice came from the back of the Cave. "Remember the words the Elders used to read to us out of the Good Book. How they took the wrongdoers outside the walls and stoned them?"

The question hung heavily in the air. Nobody spoke, but another shiver ran through the crowd.

"GO!" Jody pushed Mike Flynn and turned to face the crowd. "Don't listen to the voice of violence," he shouted, and his deep voice reverberated through the Cave. "Let violence once come to Isis and it will never leave. We will be ruled by it for ever."

"There's plenty of rocks just outside the entrance there." Chris London's voice was as loud as Jody's. He and his brothers pushed forward against the solid mass of the crowd. Their push was communicated from one row to the next, as each moved forward to keep his balance. The movement became a wave, the wave a surge. Other voices joined in the shouting.

"My hands are torn to bits digging out those damn firestones."

"And a cough that won't let me sleep nights."

"Aye, my man coughs blood too."

"All for a promise of nothing."

"He's made *fools* of us!"

The people of Isis rushed forward into the bottleneck of the entrance. It was now only that Jody's warning seemed to penetrate Mike Flynn's shocked mind. With a look of panic at the faces closing in on him he ran from the cave.

Once he had gone Jody tried to block the way. He called to his brothers and friends, and they tried to push through to help him. But anger was stronger than good sense and they were knocked down, pushed aside, trampled; and the people streamed out to wreak vengeance on the man who had come to make fools of them.

Mike Flynn had not yet reached the eastern side of the mesa when the first stone hit him, catching him just behind the knee. He slipped, yelped with pain, and limped desperately on, his eyes on the white gash of the waterfall at the head of the red valley.

Jody picked himself off the floor of the cave, shook his head clear and then ran out to overtake the mob. He came of a race slim and long-legged, and as a boy he could outrun anyone on Isis. This day he ran faster than he had ever run before, his brown legs scissoring the distance between the cave and the crumpled red and gold figure now lying among the scree.

Once he had reached him he turned, blocking the target.

Raised arms paused. Angry voices died.

"But he is only a N'Kumo," Roger London's voice whined into the silence. "And I am your President."

"Who welcomed and shared your home with this man you now want us to kill," Jody challenged him.

"I say let's stone them both," Chris yelled into the silence. "Good riddance if you ask me. Then we can go on the way we always have. The old ways. The good ways."

A stone thudded, but fell short, breaking into fragments at Jody's feet. One of the pieces drew blood from his shin, but he seemed not to notice it.

"Take care, people of Isis," he said, so softly that the people became very still in order to hear what he was saying. "You're making a choice today that can never be unmade. If you believe you can go back to the old ways through violence, you're wrong, for there was no violence on Isis in the old days."

A few stones fell to the ground, dropped, not thrown. Nobody moved, except to look sideways at his neighbour to see how *he* intended to act.

Clouds scudded across the sky on high furious winds, but on the ground the dust lay heavy and still, except for the cloud that David and Moira kicked up as they ran across the grassland from the Place within the Wall. Their feet made no sound and nobody turned or saw them.

"Oh, me stars! 'Tis Dad, and they're killing him!"

"It'll be all right. Go and tell Guardian. Run now. I'll help Uncle Jody hold them back."

She nodded and veered off to the left, running towards the western side of the mesa where Guardian had parked her flyer. She ran with a hand to her side where a stitch twisted like a knife, and she gasped with the very last of her breath.

Guardian had been dusting off the flyer in his finicky way. He stopped at once, but seemed as calm as ever. "Climb aboard," he told her. "It is fortunate that the storm did not damage the jets in any way. There is a considerable amount of paint loss, but then your craft was hardly in mint condition when it arrived, was it?"

"Guardian, they're killing him *now*," she yelled, and pushed him ahead of her into the flyer.

As David ran he suddenly remembered the weapon that Moira had shown him within the Sacred Cave. With that in his hand he could hold off the whole population of Isis. But a sense that it would not be the right thing to do held him off and he ran on, past the Cave, past the edge of the crowd, to come to a panting halt beside his uncle.

"No, David. Get out of here," Jody's voice was low, but urgent.

"It's my fight too."

"Because of the girl? What is she to you?"

"I'd marry her tomorrow if she'd only have me."

"Sure and you'd be a lovely boy for me own darling." Mike Flynn's voice was muffled by his arms, which were wrapped protectingly around his head and neck as he crouched on the turf.

"David is an N'Kumo too." Chris's voice was loud, urging them on. "Let's take care of all three of them. And the girl too, if we can lay hands on her."

"Her most of all." Charlie had twisted her arm just a little bit as they'd dragged her out of the London house, and the hell-cat had actually bitten him. She owed him for that bite.

The mood of the crowd changed again. It was like a storm on the lake. The wind could beat the water into a froth, sending waves up almost to the edge of the village, and then subsiding into a temporary calm before the next gust. Yet, in storm or calm, it was still the same water within the lake.

David looked at the angry faces and shivered inside. They were his friends, his relatives, many of them. But they no longer looked like individuals. Their anger was a mask, making all of them look alike. He was very much afraid.

Uncle Jody caught his eye in that instant's shivering, and smiled. Just a fleeting smile, but in it he knew that they shared the same feelings, the same fear. Suddenly it became almost easy to face the anger and even the stones of the mob, to protect a man whom he despised.

Into that instant, when the crowd teetered between violence and peace, tore a scream. Everyone turned. There were other screams. People pointing. The crowd broke apart into people turning to run.

David and Jody turned to the north-east in time to see the silver flyer bank gently between the mesa and the river valley wall, and come to rest on the turf. It landed in a cloud of red dust, and there came walking out of it the golden figure of the Guardian, with Moira by his side.

David stared. How beautiful she looks, and how proudly she walks. Her father boasts of being descended from the kings of old Ireland. Maybe it is true. Certainly she is like a queen. He longed to run forward to meet her, to gather her in his arms and tell every last soul on Isis that he loved her. But he didn't move.

Beside him Jody also stood motionless. Their calm seemed to spread to those around them. People stopped running, turned, and stood. They stayed in groups, well back, for safety's sake, and watched with open mouths as the Guardian and the girl walked slowly towards the stranger and the N'Kumos.

When Moira reached David's side she smiled and slipped her hand into his. Guardian walked on, stiff-legged, to stand above the huddled shape of Mike Flynn, who, after one look, had buried his head in his arms again.

"Stand up, Michael Flynn!"

Something in the voice made Mike scramble to his feet.

"Look at me."

Reluctantly Mike turned. "Why, you're only a . . ."

The crystal eyes flashed and everyone saw the stranger flinch and turn even paler. They all saw his knees tremble and his skinny body sag. It was Jody N'Kumo who stepped forward and grasped his arm, to keep him on his feet. They could all see that there had never been any power in the stranger, only words and tricks.

Everyone saw something else, something that they had refused to recognise before—the strength that was in Jody N'Kumo, who had grown into a leader of men in the years since he had come back to the valley after his banishment.

Guardian spoke to the shrinking stranger. "Do you know who I am?"

Mike Flynn made a strange whinnying noise and shook his head. It went on trembling like that of an old man.

"I am the Guardian of Isis."

A shiver went through the people. They began to kneel, but he put up a hand to stop them.

"This man is not from Isis," Guardian explained to the people. "I did not send him to you. He came out of space to prey on you, and I am going to send him back where he belongs. You must not touch him. Go back to your houses. Repair what the storm has damaged. Tomorrow you must continue the harvesting. It will be a hard job for you this year, since you neglected it in the proper season, and now the storm has flattened the stalks."

111

They looked from one to another, shame-faced, and were relieved when Guardian dismissed them with another gesture of his golden hand. It was wonderful to see, all right, but more comfortable to turn away, to turn one's thoughts to talking about the harvest and speculating on how much damage had been done.

Now and then, once they were safely across the river, they turned round as they walked, as if to admire the sunset, which was indeed most vivid after the storm. As they looked at the view they could also see the figures of young David and the strange girl with black hair, standing very close together. More astonishing was the sight of Jody N'Kumo, who had been of no account at all in the past, holding the golden hands of Guardian, just as if they were old friends meeting after a long separation.

Apart from them, very small and insignificant in his dusty clothes, was the forlorn figure of the stranger, Michael Joseph Flynn.

Once they'd got back to the village the London boys went silently off to help the others clean up the debris of the storm-damaged houses. They said not a single word to their father. Neither did their mother. Only, as soon as Roger London was inside the door of his house, she snatched the quilt that he had been using as a cloak from his shoulders, shook the dust from it with remarkable ferocity for a meek woman, and put it back on the bed where it belonged.

Nothing more was ever said about the matter of the Stranger in the London house, but Emma London had a way of glaring at that same quilt any time she thought he was getting 'uppity' that silenced Roger London completely.

Chapter Ten

"I didn't mean a particle of harm, and that's the truth."
Mike Flynn's eyes were wide and guileless. The people
sitting at the tables in the dining hall began to find
themselves believing him again. He went on again eagerly.
"It's like the drink, your honour. An idea grabs hold of me
and it's such a beautiful thing, such a grand notion entirely,
that I have to see it through, no matter what."

Jody N'Kumo's eyes twinkled, though his face remained
stern. He sat in the President's chair now, following the
resignation of Roger London. Even London's sons hadn't
opposed him. Now he leaned forward to question Mike
Flynn. "An idea? Wasn't it really just greed that spurred you
on. Greed for riches beyond your wildest dreams?"

"Nothing is beyond the scope of my dreams." The pedlar
drew himself up to his full height as if he'd just been
insulted. "My dreams are magnificent, all-embracing. Why,
even here on Isis I can see such a splendid future for you if
you will only . . ."

"No!" Jody's voice cut through the flamboyance.

"No? It seems a pity now. Why, your power in the
Galaxy . . ."

"Our destiny is our own, and we'll work it out without
interference. Listen well, Michael Joseph Flynn. We, the
people of Isis, have talked together about what punishment
you should be given for all you have done."

"Ah, now, surely, your honour, it wasn't that bad, and no harm done in the long run."

"No thanks to you. If Guardian had not been able to treat the ill effects of mountain sickness you might have murder on your conscience too. Our decision is this: to send you away from Isis, never to return. You may smile, but we can think of no worse punishment. And you will forfeit the firestones you brought with you, as well as those you got from us."

"That's not just at all! Didn't I win them honestly in a game of . . ."

"Oh, Dad, will you shut your mouth!" Moira burst out.

Jody raised his hand. "You'll give us every last one, and we'll search you to be sure. I don't want the risk of one of them turning up in a bar on some other planet, with a wild story about the place where they can be found as thick as fruit in a Thanksgiving Day pudding. Without the stones you have no story, and you won't be tempted to talk about Isis. And that is our second condition: silence. We intend to have a good and happy place here. You brought us lies and greed. I don't want that to happen again."

"You'll amount to nothing at all if you cut yourselves off from the rest of the Galaxy, and I'm telling you that for your own good."

"I'm sure. And I tell you: we'll reach out when *we're* ready, and not before. Now stand up, Michael Joseph Flynn, and face the people whom you have wronged. In the name of the people of Isis I banish you from our planet and demand that you swear never to mention this place to a living soul."

"Certainly, your honour. Whatever you say, I'm sure."

"You will leave tomorrow at Ra-up. That is all. You may go."

Feeling very small and wretched Moira followed her father through the crowd of silent eyes back towards the N'Kumo house where they were lodged. Someone touched her arm. It was David.

"Come. I'll see you to the house."

She smiled at him with gratitude, her eyes sparkling with tears.

"And now to the harvest!" Jody called to the rest of the people. "What's done is in the past. We have the winter to think of, so back to work."

His scythe flashed alongside the others, and the sweat ran down his naked back too, as the day grew warm and they worked on. It was only during the rest period that he left his place among the other men and crossed the river to tell Guardian what had been decided.

"I hope I spoke wisely this morning," he said. "There is so much to do, so much that must be changed. I don't know where to begin."

"Be slow," Guardian told him. "Remember what I said to you long ago when you were a boy, younger than David. The wind and the rain and the river carved out your valley over millions of years. Your time here has been no more than a breath in the life of Isis. Be patient, Jody, my friend. Work like water on a stone, not like fire in a thorn bush."

"I'll try—with your help. You *will* stay in the valley and help me, won't you? Now the people know exactly what you are, what's the harm?"

"Government by Guardian, instead of government by an elected Council? Would that be a step forward?"

"Only your advice, so I won't make mistakes."

"Jody, to be human is to make mistakes."

"Like Mike Flynn?"

"No indeed. He doesn't learn from his mistakes. He spins them into lies and victories. You can do better than that. You'll learn from your mistakes and grow."

"So you won't stay? You'll go back to Bamboo Valley?"

"I won't stay. To the people I am still uncomfortably like a god. Better out of sight."

"Was that why you stayed in the flyer instead of coming into the village? Oh, Guardian, I thought that perhaps after Olwen's death you couldn't bear people."

115

"Ah." Guardian was silent. Then he said slowly, "No indeed. Sometimes I feel a kind of hunger. To be useful, to be loved."

"Then stay."

But Guardian would only shake his head and say no more, and it was time for Jody to go back to the harvesting.

That night after supper the N'Kumo family lingered as usual around a small thornbush fire in the living room of the family house. It was a silent gathering, and for once even Mike seemed to have nothing to say. One by one the family said goodnight and left for bed, until David and Moira were alone, sitting close together by the dying fire.

Moira sighed.

"Are you tired?" David asked.

"No. And I don't want to waste this last night in sleep and that's the truth of it."

"Let's go outside then. Here, this cloak is big enough for both of us." He wrapped it over their shoulders and, arms around each other, they went out and climbed the slope beside the cemetery. In the brilliant starlight the crosses gleamed.

"It is strange to think that all the people who have ever lived on this planet are buried in this one small spot."

"It is strange to hear you speak of Isis as 'planet', as if there were other places where people were living."

"But there are."

"Oh, I understand that now. But it is still strange. Will you be glad to be gone? To travel from star to star out there?"

She didn't answer, and when he touched her face it was wet with tears.

"What is it?"

"Oh, David. I don't want to leave and that's the simple truth. The thought is killing me."

"Then *stay*. Marry me, Moira. You know how much I love you."

"I can't. It's not my place, is it?"

116

"It could be. They will love you too, and you've got so much to offer us. You could teach the young ones to read and write."

"Oh, I'd like that fine!"

"You could teach us about space and science."

"Do you need all that, do you think? You were happy enough without it."

"Would we have fallen for your father's tricks if we'd been a little wiser?"

She laughed scornfully. "He's fooled many a so-called educated man before now. But perhaps you're right. If wisdom *can* be taught as well as book learning, it might be a good thing."

"Then stay. We all need you. Not just me, all of us."

"I cannot. Oh David, do not torment me with asking. Let's just sit here on the turf and breathe the clean untroubled air and watch the stars move until morning. Let me have just that to remember, David."

He tilted her face up until he could see it in the starlight, her eyes shining with tears, her hair vanishing in the darkness of night. "It's that promise you made your mother, isn't it?"

She nodded.

"He's not worth it, Moira my love."

"I know it. That's why I must keep the promise, can you not see that? If he were a good man he wouldn't need me. I wouldn't have to be there to get him out of scrapes and look after him, the way my Mam did. But he'll hold me to that promise till his dying day, I know it. He's weak. But he's my father, and in a way I love him."

"Perhaps if you let him go his own way he'd grow up."

"I've thought of that. But suppose he doesn't? If he ruins himself and others too, it'll be my fault then, won't it?"

"No, Moira. He's your father, not your child."

"Sometimes I wonder and that's the truth." She gave a soft half-laugh, half-sob. Then she leaned back against his

117

chest and looked up at the sky. "Such beauty. Please, David, share it with me and torment me no more."

They sat in silence above the sleeping houses, while the stars moved and faded. David watched Moira's face as the sky grew lighter and he could see the details he wanted never to forget: the eyelashes thick and black, the scatter of tiny freckles across the bridge of her nose. She dozed quietly against his shoulder, and he felt that never could he know so much joy and so much pain at one time.

The stars went out one by one. She woke shivering and he held her close under the cloak until she was warm again. Then it was time to go.

They walked slowly down to meet Jody and Mike Flynn. Together the four of them walked up river to the stepping stones and then across the storm-flattened grass to the flyer that waited like a resting moth on the turf below the dark bulk of Lighthouse Mesa.

The closer they got to the flyer the more sprightly Mike Flynn's step became and the cheerier his conversation. "Are you raring for a new adventure, me darling? How about a visit to a grand up-to-date planet with good food and fine clothes?"

"Whatever you want, Dad," Moira said listlessly.

"Whatever you want, Dad!" He mimicked her. His pale eyes sparkled. "Sure and that's a thrilling response. 'Tis a grand companion you're likely to be for the next while. You'd better stay here since you like it so well."

She bit her lip. Sometimes his teasing moods were the worst. He had a knack of getting right under her skin. "I've told you I'll keep my promise, Dad. I'll stay with you as long as you want me."

"Then listen, girl." He twisted her out of David's arms and held her in front of him. "I don't want you. I'd rather travel alone in me own harumscarum way than have you moping and mothering me to death."

"Oh, Dad, stop your nonsense, will you? How could you manage alone? You can't even repair the drive!"

118

"But *I* can." Guardian had been waiting for them by the flyer. Now he spoke, almost eagerly for a robot. "Oh, I know I'm old-fashioned annd sometimes forgetful, but I have the capacity to repair the drive and navigate and play poker and cook and . . ."

Moira was crying and laughing at the same time. She looked from Guardian to Mike. "Do you really mean it, Guardian? Do you truly want to go with him?"

"To travel through the Galaxy, to learn new languages and customs, to see things that are not in my program . . ." He stopped and turned to Mike. "I must confess that my programming is sadly out of date, but I am sure that can be remedied. In expert hands, who knows what I might be capable of. Oh, to be young again!" His crystal eyes sparkled.

"Would it work?" Moira turned to her father. "You'd miss me sorely, Mike. You'll be lonely out there in the empty places between."

"If you'll excuse the interruption," Guardian said firmly. "My prime programming is in the area of companionship. Really," he added modestly, "I am the perfect friend."

Mike Flynn began to laugh and broke into a sudden leap-kick as if he were about to dance. "And I'll not tire of you, Guardian, if you'll not tire of me. What an idea! Oh, the lovely times we'll have. The things we can do—with my imagination and your brains!"

"Oh, Dad, no! Haven't you learned anything here?"

"Do not worry, Moira. He will do nothing that you would not approve of."

"It's that way, is it?" Mike pouted. "Maybe I'll be having second thoughts about taking you along. Though how you're to guess what me daughter would approve of, I'm at a loss to know."

"I will measure what you do against Olwen's approval. I always know how *she* would have felt. Will that satisfy you, Moira?"

"Oh, yes."

"And you, Michael Joseph Flynn, will you accept me on those terms?"

"You won't be spoiling the good times entirely?"

"No."

"And you'll not stop me having the wee tot once in a while?"

"As long as your health permits."

"And you will not be forever complaining and wanting to settle down and raise a family?"

"Oh, *Dad*!" Moira protested, blushing.

"Then it's a bargain. Oh, Moira, me darling, it's no good. I've two itchy feet and a Galaxy before me. I'm nothing but a pedlar with a magic pack on me back and planets galore ahead of me. I'm a wanderer and I'll be that till they bury me, and then me soul will probably go on wandering too."

"It sounds like a most stimulating program." Guardian nodded his head and his eyes flashed more brilliantly than ever.

"So we'll be off then. Let's waste no time on goodbyes. Moira, me love, is there anything you want from the ship before we go into hyperspace?"

"No, Dad. I've the locket Mam gave me, and there's nothing else that I can't find down here."

"Then I'll be asking you for me force field belt back, if you'll be so kind as to tell me where the devil you've hid it."

They couldn't help laughing at Mike's assurance and the comical expression on his face. At a nod from Jody David ran to bring both belts from the Cave.

"But I had them searching in there. I even looked myself."

"Did you look in the water jug?"

"It hadn't been touched. The dust . . ." Mike broke off, and slapped David on the shoulder. "Oh, but you're the smart one. You've outfoxed Michael Joseph Flynn, and there are few enough have ever done that! Sure and I feel happier leaving me only daughter with a man who could get the better of Mike Flynn. Take her then, and bless you both."

He turned and climbed quickly into the flyer. Guardian made more leisurely goodbyes.

"Take care of him."

"I promise you that, as I loved Olwen, so will I love your father."

"I couldn't ask for more. Thank you. And take care of yourself too."

"Oh, we DaCoPs are indestructible." Guardian stopped abruptly, and for an instant his eyes were opaque, inward looking. Then he went on as if nothing had happened. "When you leave this valley, as you will one day, and settle in the other valleys of Isis, will you look after her pool and her grave?"

"I will, Guardian. I promise." She stood on tiptoe and touched her lips to his smooth gold cheek.

"Come on then," Mike called impatiently. "In you get, Guardian. No time to waste. Goodbye, Moira, me love. I'll be back to see you some day."

The door was sealed, and David and Moira and Jody hurried back to the river. On the far side every person on Isis had come out to see the Pedlar leave.

The flyer took off in a flare of rockets, and banked in a curve around the mesa. Level with the old Light it caught the rays of the rising sun and turned to brilliant silver, so that everyone blinked or turned away. When they could look again it was only a dot.

"Goodbye, Mike," Moira whispered. "I'll miss you and that's the truth."

The three of them crossed the river and walked back to the village after the others in the growing light.

"Do you think he meant what he said—about coming back some day?"

"I hope not." David laughed and hugged her to take the sting from the words. "Once in a lifetime's enough!"